IN A HEARTBEAT

Kayla Perrin

BET Publications, LLC
http://www.bet.com
http://www.arabesquebooks.com

ARABESQUE BOOKS are published by

BET Publications, LLC
c/o BET BOOKS
One BET Plaza
1900 W Place NE
Washington, DC 20018-1211

All Kensington Titles, Imprints, and Distributed Lines are available at special quantity discounts for bulk purchases for sales promotions, premiums, fund-raising, and educational or institutional use. Special book excerpts or customized printings can also be created to fit specific needs. For details, write or phone the office of the Kensington special sales manager: Kensington Publishing Corp., 850 Third Avenue, New York, NY 10022, attn: Special Sales Department, Phone: 1-800-221-2647.

First Printing: April 2003
10 9 8 7 6 5 4 3 2 1

Printed in the United States of America

For Uncle Denny and Peaches.
You two have proven that
true love will always win out
in the end.

CHAPTER ONE

Diamond Montgomery clenched the steering wheel, fear churning in her stomach like acid. She was speeding, she knew, but she didn't care. The faster she got out of town, the better.

Even if she had no clue where she was going.

She only knew that she needed to get away. Far enough that he wouldn't find her.

A shaky breath escaped her as the detective's message played in her mind like a record. *There's no way to tell you this, Diamond. Clay has escaped.*

Escaped. God help her.

But hadn't she sensed it? During the past year, she had started receiving weird calls and letters at her workplace, radio station Talk 93 in South Florida. Every call and letter had reminded her of the incident with Clay Horton, an obsessed fan who ultimately had tried to abduct her. And as much as she had tried to keep her wits about her— knowing Clay was locked up in a mental facility— she had started to unravel, wondering what was going on. Wondering if she had a new and equally deranged and dangerous stalker with whom to contend.

After a near-fatal car crash as she'd fled her apartment because a package from the stalker had arrived there, Diamond had been completely devastated to learn that Paul, her live-in police officer boyfriend, had been behind all the letters and phone calls. He had been determined to see her quit her popular radio show, even if he'd had to scare her half to death to do so. Of course, knowing how close she'd come to possibly losing her life, Paul had regretted his immature actions. He'd apologized and Diamond had accepted the apology. Then she had moved out of his apartment and moved on with her life.

She should have felt better once that was all resolved, but she hadn't. For months, she had continued to feel jittery every time she left the radio station and walked to her car, every time she opened a letter from a fan.

Without cause, it had seemed—until now.

Because now, Clay had escaped. And she had no doubt that he was coming after her.

I don't want to alarm you, the detective had said, *but the staff found a box in his room that contained photos of you, newspaper clippings . . .*

Diamond shook her head, trying to toss the detective's words from her mind. Paul had tried to scare her into quitting the show, convinced that she was continuing to put herself in harm's way by being a controversial public figure. She had disagreed with him—but maybe he was right.

The problem was, Diamond loved her job. She gave people advice about their relationships on her show, *The Love Chronicles.* Her words were always straightforward and to the point, and despite their sometimes controversial nature, people appreciated what she had to say. It wasn't a job she wanted to give up.

But now . . .

Diamond glanced in her rearview mirror. Seeing that there wasn't a car behind her for at least thirty feet, she eased her foot off the gas pedal. There was no need to keep up her high rate of speed. She was out of the immediate Miami area, heading west on Alligator Alley, and from what she could tell, she wasn't being followed.

Not that she expected to be followed. Yet her heart raced as though Clay were in a car right behind her.

Relax, she told herself.

But how could she? Her car was filled with items from her apartment, enough that she could start over somewhere else. She was preparing for the worst, while hoping for the best. Without warning, her life had been pulled out from under her.

Diamond had barely had a chance to call her station manager and let him know what was going on. "I'm leaving," she'd told him. "Clay's escaped and he's coming for me."

"Diamond, go to the police. Let them take care of you."

"Like they did the first time?" Diamond had sighed, knowing Ken cared about her and was worried about her. And normally she would agree— let the police handle things. But Clay had proved to be too clever for the police the first time, and Diamond would have been his victim, had it not been for two passersby who had come to her rescue as Clay had wrestled with her, trying to stuff her into his car.

She could not go through something like that again.

As she drove along Alligator Alley, she glanced out at the Everglades. Beyond the fence at the side of the road was a length of water that ran along the highway for miles. Some days, you could see several alligators swimming in the water, or getting sun on the water's edge. Hence, this stretch of I-75 had been named Alligator Alley.

But today, Diamond looked and saw nothing. She was preoccupied.

Damn Clay.

As Lady D, talk radio show host, Diamond was used to fans. She had many. Some were outspoken on the various topics she discussed on her popular show. Not everyone who called in agreed with her—mostly the men, who sometimes accused her of being biased—but that was the way she wanted it. Controversy was good. Controversy kept the ratings high.

Other callers seemed to think she walked on water, dishing out only praise for whatever opinion she expressed on the topic of male-female relationships.

It was a show she had enjoyed hosting over the past years, and it had garnered her a lot of attention. Unfortunately, some people who listened to her show were a few sandwiches short of a picnic basket. Clay was one of them.

Clay had started off writing letters. The first ones had seemed harmless, but the more he sent, the bolder he became. Soon, he was telling her what he wanted to do to her in explicit sexual detail. After the letters came the calls to the radio station, calls that always gave her the creeps.

He had progressed from letters and calls to sending her gifts. She'd known she was in trouble when she started finding cards from him on the windshield of her car.

She had reported it all to the police, who, in effect, could only wait until Clay struck. No one knew his last name, and he never called from a number that could be identified. Therefore, he couldn't be found. And for all anyone knew, he was using a fake name.

Whoever he was, Diamond had always known that it would be only a matter of time before he struck.

Just like she knew that his escape from the mental facility a couple of days ago meant he was coming to find her.

She could be nowhere near Miami now. And she definitely would not return until Clay was caught and put in a room with rubber walls from which he would never escape.

Damn his sister.

Michael Robbins drove west toward his Naples home at a steady clip on I-75, frustration brimming inside him. He should have known that Kelly's call to him had been exaggerated—to put it kindly. Lately, his sister tended to exaggerate everything that was going on in her life, which shouldn't have surprised him, even if it disappointed him. Her boss wasn't annoying—he was a first-class sexist jerk. Her coworkers weren't simply flighty—they were back-stabbing haters. And the men she met— well, according to Kelly, they were either totally possessive or totally clueless.

All her life, she had been a drama queen, but she had had other people besides him to pull into the drama. Like her friends. Therefore, Michael had never truly been affected by it. On occasion, he would overhear her speaking with a friend in her bedroom about some guy who had broken her heart, but she had never come to him with her problems. Now, however, that was all Kelly did. At a time when she knew that he preferred to be left alone, she called constantly to complain about one thing or another in her life.

And to get him to listen or to call her back, she usually resorted to tears.

Michael wouldn't mind her antics so much if he hadn't become the focus of them. There was no way that Kelly had that much drama going on. But his sister seemed to feel that the way to lure him out of his shell was to involve him more in her life—even if that meant creating reasons to call him. She was on some sort of charity mission to make his life better, right all the wrongs he had suffered.

Kelly wanted him to move back to Southeast Florida. She figured he was pretty much living as a hermit in Naples—which he was. Time and again he told her that he wasn't moving back, at least not yet. So she resorted to other ways to get him out of the house to visit her, like her stunt today. This was her way of making sure that he was all right.

Even as Michael had driven the two hours to her place this time, he had wondered if she was pulling his leg. "He won't leave me alone," Kelly had said. "I know I heard him outside my apartment last night. Please, Michael. Won't you come and stay with me for a little while?"

Michael hadn't been willing to gamble on the fact that his sister was stretching the truth, at least not when it concerned an obsessive ex. However, when he arrived at Kelly's apartment and found that she had set him up to meet a female friend of his, he had not been impressed.

Angry was more like it.

Michael groaned, tightening his hand on the steering wheel. He loved his sister—he truly did—but she was deluded where he was concerned. He didn't need a "good woman" in his life to help him get over the pains of his past. The only thing that would heal his tortured soul was some space and time for himself. Space and time where he could reflect on what had happened and finally get over it.

"It's been six months, Michael," his sister had said when he'd arrived at her apartment and was furious to learn that she had lied to him. "Why haven't you forgiven yourself?"

It was easy for her to ask, but she wasn't the one who had to live with the constant nightmares. Everyone said that time would heal all wounds, but so far, time hadn't been kind to him.

Neither had the Fort Lauderdale Police. Michael scowled, remembering yet another incident in his life that had gone terribly wrong. Once he'd been suspended from the force, he had known that things would never be the same. During the Internal Affairs investigation, he'd made what some people had considered a rash decision and retired from the force. He much preferred retiring in lieu of continuing and having everyone second-guess every decision he made—even if Internal Affairs had ultimately cleared him of any wrongdoing.

In the end, his captain had convinced him to take an extended leave of absence.

Then, Michael knew that the loss of his daughter

and wife seven months earlier had made everyone concerned, and he couldn't entirely blame them. They weren't sure how well he was holding himself together. So, when the shooting had taken place, even his captain had wondered if his judgment had been clouded because of his personal problems.

Which had hurt. Because in the six years that Michael had been on the force, he'd had an impeccable record.

Taking an extended leave of absence had been the right choice for him, one he didn't regret. Over the past months, he had come to enjoy his solitude. He certainly preferred his quiet home in Naples to the populated apartment complex where he had lived in Fort Lauderdale.

And ever since his year from hell, he found that people annoyed him. More so, it was too difficult to watch everyone around him laughing and having a good time, while he was still suffering his most devastating loss. Who knew? Maybe he wouldn't go back to the force. The way he had left the military and not looked back.

Then, he hadn't questioned his decision. The night that one of his best friends was injured in Desert Storm and he hadn't been able to airlift him to safety in time, still haunted him. After returning home, Michael had decided that he wanted to pursue another line of work—one where he didn't have to witness his friends dying, or fear they'd soon be killed. A job where he still helped others, but didn't deal with horrors every day. The natural answer had been to join the police force.

But that hadn't worked out, either.

Over his past months of solitude, he had come to realize that there was a pattern to his life—things just didn't work out. No matter what it was, something went wrong. There was that horrible day during the Gulf War, his marriage ... his daughter. He fought the sting of tears. And finally, there had been the shooting six months ago.

Maybe he was cursed, or paying for sins from another lifetime. Surely he couldn't be this unlucky.

"Forget it all," Michael told himself. Pushing the memories to the back of his mind, he gazed out at the Everglades as he drove. Concentrating on the lush view, he breathed in and out slowly, forcing himself to relax.

Minutes later, he was feeling better. This world was much more peaceful than the zoo that was South Florida, and did a lot for calming his nerves. He was glad to be on his way back home. He wouldn't let Kelly con him into the two-hour drive again. He was tired of her games.

Glancing into the rearview mirror, he saw a car behind him to his left. Other than that, traffic was fairly sparse. Yet something made his stomach coil with tension, and he continued to gaze in the rearview mirror for the next several moments.

He realized what was bothering him. The black Acura behind him seemed to be speeding up, then slowing down. Great. Was this guy drunk? Drunks were unpredictable.

Michael continued to eye the car. Something definitely wasn't right with how the driver was moving on the road.

Michael looked ahead on the straight stretch of road, then once again viewed the car behind him. The car sped up, inching toward his.

Michael's stomach plummeted with horror. The car veered suddenly to the right, and he knew, in an instant, that it would collide with his.

Gripping the steering wheel, Michael turned to the right, but it was too late to avoid an accident. The offending car smashed into his with a loud crash and a bump that propelled him forward on an angle.

"For the love of God!" Michael exclaimed. Gritting his teeth, he slowed down, maneuvering his car onto the shoulder. All the while he kept an eye on the driver who had hit him. In case he took off, he wanted to be able to get the guy's license plate number.

But the other car slowed as well, pulling onto the shoulder behind him. At least the driver wasn't fleeing the scene.

Fully stopped, Michael slammed his car into park and jumped out. He barely threw the other driver a glance as he made his way to the back of his vehicle to inspect it for damage.

"Great. Just friggin' great." The left side of his bumper was completely smashed. And the Honda was less than a year old.

Michael whipped his head around to see that the driver of the car was now standing mere feet from him. He felt a moment of shock, noticing that the driver was a woman. She flinched, which made him realize that the expression he wore must have been one that could kill.

"I-I," she stuttered, but couldn't get anything beyond that from her lips.

"What were you thinking?" Michael bellowed. He couldn't contain his anger, not when this had been so senseless.

"I'm sorry. I just—"

"Just what?"

She bit down on her lower lip, clearly distressed. "I didn't mean to."

"The road was clear," Michael went on. "Very little traffic. I don't know why you decided to change lanes, anyway." *Just like a woman,* he wanted to add, but didn't. "What were you doing, putting on makeup?" The question was sexist, but as a cop, he had stopped a fair number of women doing just that. And considering those lush lips of hers were perfectly covered with dark lipstick, he figured he was pretty much right on the mark.

But the woman's eyes registered shock, like his comment was insulting. Then she shook her head briskly, as though she didn't have a voice to speak. Michael stared at her, wondering what on earth was wrong with her.

Her lower lip trembled beneath his assessing gaze, and then she turned away, covering her face with a hand.

Great. Just great. She'd smashed into him, and now she was the one crying. His sister had pulled this stunt more times than he could count, and he hoped this wasn't a ploy to get out of paying him for the damage.

Michael asked, "You have insurance, don't you?"

The woman took a moment to compose herself, faced him, and replied, "Yes. Of course."

"All right." Michael's tone was softer. "Then there's no need to get all upset. No one's going to arrest you."

The woman wiped at her eyes. "You don't understand."

"What don't I understand?" Michael suddenly got the feeling that something more was going on with this woman, something other than her merely being distressed over hitting his car.

He took a closer look at her. She had beautiful, bright eyes, eyes that were filled with fear.

Because of him?

He doubted it.

"Look, I just . . ." She sighed. "Give me your information, and I'll make sure I pay for the damage."

"Are you okay?" Michael asked her.

She shot him a startled gaze.

Michael took a step closer to her. Yeah, there was definitely something else going on with her. He'd been around enough women in distress to know.

"You look in no condition to be driving," he added.

"I can drive," she quickly responded. "I have to . . ."

His cop instincts went on high alert. Was this woman running from something? And if so, what? Had she broken some law? Or was something else going on?

Michael asked, "Where are you going?"

"Why does that matter?"

"Because I'm concerned about you."

The woman eyed him warily. "You think I'm not going to pay you."

"No, I'm worried about you continuing to drive if your state of mind isn't right." And it wasn't. It was clear just by looking at her that her mind was a million miles away.

The woman headed back to her car door, and Michael quickly followed her. He wasn't about to let her drive off in the middle of their conversation, especially not in her state. As she climbed behind the wheel, he took hold of the door so she couldn't close it.

She reached for a pad of paper and a pen, scribbled something on the sheet, then passed it to him.

"This is who I am. And this is where you can reach me."

Michael took the sheet of paper and examined it. Her name was Diamond. That was different, but he sensed it suited her to a T. "Miami?" he asked, recognizing the area code.

"Yes."

"And where are you going again?"

"You're asking a lot of questions."

"I want to make sure this isn't a bogus number."

"I'm just . . ." She bit down on her bottom lip and glanced over her shoulder.

Exactly whom was she expecting to see out here on this stretch of highway?

"You don't know where you're going, do you?" It wasn't a question. Michael didn't know why, but his gut told him this was a woman in trouble. His gut, and experience.

"I need to get away. Far away," she added softly. Diamond climbed out of the car and walked around to the front. She stooped to inspect the damage. She fingered the large dent, groaning. "This is going to need some serious repairs. And the light's shot to hell." She shook her head. "With the amount of money this car cost, I would think it could withstand a little bump."

"It wasn't that little."

Diamond slowly rose. "I'm sorry. I don't mean to be so concerned about myself. The last thing I wanted to do was hit you or anyone else. I really am sorry."

"What's done is done."

She nodded, then hugged her torso. Once again, Michael couldn't help thinking that this woman was in trouble.

He had never believed in karma, but maybe he

should start. The universe was clearly sending him a message, always sending women in need into his life.

That was how he'd met his wife, Debra. An image of her when he had pulled her over for speeding, scared and trembling, filled his mind. That was five years ago. The instant he saw her, Michael's protective instincts kicked in. It turned out Debra had been running from a bad marriage. At least that's what she'd told him. Now, given everything, he couldn't be sure her words that first day were true. Because during her time with him, she had proven to be everything but the meek and scared woman in need of protection she had first made herself out to be.

But this wasn't Debra, he reminded himself. This was Diamond. If he washed his hands of the situation and let this woman go on wherever she was going, what would happen to her?

"Why don't you follow me?" he suggested, the words a surprise to his own ears. At her startled look, he added, "It's obvious you're in some kind of trouble, and at my place, you can at least lie low for a while. At least until you figure out what you want to do and where you want to be going."

"That's completely unnecessary," Diamond told him.

"Diamond?" Michael said, asking for confirmation of her name.

"Yes, Diamond."

He extended a hand. "My name is Michael."

She regarded his hand a few seconds before accepting it. "Hello, Michael."

"There. We're no longer strangers." He smiled, but she merely gave him a wary look in return.

"Look, Diamond. I insist that you follow me. The

last thing I want to do is abandon a woman in trouble.''

She gazed up at him, her eyes gleaming. She really did have beautiful eyes. They were light brown and had an intriguing sparkle.

"Are you a cop?" she asked.

Michael actually chuckled. "That's a pretty good guess. Yeah. I guess I am.''

"You guess?"

"I'm on a leave of absence.''

"I knew you were a cop." She smirked, clearly satisfied with herself. "You have that look.''

Silence fell between them, stretching for several seconds. Michael was the first to speak. "I'm a cop. You know you can trust me.''

"Ha!"

"Excuse me?"

"My ex is a cop. And straight-up crazy. But that's another story.''

Is it the ex who's crazy, or you? Michael couldn't help wondering. But he said, "I assure you, I'm not in the habit of picking up women in distress.'' Well, that wasn't entirely true. "I figure you need some time to cool down, get yourself composed. Maybe even think about what it is you're doing. You can do that at my place.''

Michael saw the hesitation in her eyes.

"Why are you on leave?" she asked.

"And you said I ask a lot of questions.''

"Something you don't want to tell me?"

"It has nothing to do with whether or not you can trust me. Something bad happened. I needed a break.''

"For all I know, you were fired from the force for criminal activity.''

"Then I'd be in jail.''

"Not if you were too smart for everyone." But she actually gave him a smile, letting him know she was teasing him.

"Touché. But not true. So, what do you—"

Michael stopped in midsentence as he watched Diamond glance around again, watched her body stiffen as a car passed on the opposite side of the highway.

Suddenly, she was charging to the passenger side of his vehicle and yanking the door open. Locked, the door wouldn't budge.

"What the heck?" Michael said.

"Oh, God. That car on the other side of the road. It's slowing down, like he wants to turn around on the highway." Her voice was a horrified whisper. "Please. You have to get me out of here."

"Lady, what is going on?"

"There's no time to explain! Open the door. Please!"

Michael rushed to his door and opened it, then pressed the button to open the passenger door. They both scrambled into the car.

"Drive!" Diamond instructed. "You have to lose him."

CHAPTER TWO

Michael pressed the gas pedal to the floor and whipped into the right lane. The car went from zero to eighty in ten seconds flat, whizzing by every car in the immediate area.

Michael drove for a good thirty seconds before turning to Diamond and saying, "Lady, what the devil kind of trouble are you in?"

Diamond turned in her seat, twisting her neck around to survey the road behind them. "I think we lost him." She faced him. "We lost him, right?"

"I have no clue who you're talking about. All I know is that you jumped in my car and said drive."

"He was in a blue Neon, right? Or was it a black sedan? Gosh, I don't even know."

"You don't know which car it was?"

"I . . . I only saw his face. At least I thought I saw his face. Maybe I didn't."

"You force me into my car in hysterics and you're not even sure you really saw this person you're so afraid of?"

Diamond whimpered. "It's been a very stressful day."

"Tell me about it," Michael muttered.

Again, Diamond looked over her shoulder to see the road behind her. "The blue car . . . I think it's gaining on us. Can you hit the gas?"

"I'm already speeding."

"Please!"

Wondering what he had gotten himself into, Michael hit the gas, taking the car much further over the posted limit. Soon, all the cars behind them were in the very far distance.

Only when he rounded a slight curve and the cars could no longer be seen behind them did Diamond face forward once again.

"I know this is bizarre," Diamond said, casting a glance in Michael's direction. "Sorry."

"Sorry?" Michael sounded incredulous. "I think you ought to be saying a lot more than that."

Diamond heaved a weary sigh and looked at the profile of the stranger whose car she had hit. "It's a crazy story."

"I've got time."

"I think," she began slowly, knowing she owed Michael some explanation, "someone was following me. I'm pretty sure I saw him, and that's why I jumped in your car."

"Let me guess. Your ex-boyfriend?"

"No. Not an ex."

" 'No, not an ex'? That's all you're going to say?" He gave her a look that said he thought she had a couple of screws loose. More than a couple. "Please tell me you haven't dragged me into anything illegal. Man, that would be just my luck."

"Illegal? God, no. I think that was Clay."

"Who is Clay?"

"A deranged fan."

Michael shot her a skeptical look.

"I work as a radio talk show host," she explained. "Lady D of *The Love Chronicles*." He gave her a blank look, and Diamond was a little surprised that he hadn't heard of her. Practically every African-American between the ages of twenty and forty-five knew her name. But then, if he was on this stretch of I-75, he likely didn't live in Southeast Florida.

"Sorry to burst your bubble, lady, but I've never heard of you."

Diamond waved a dismissive hand. "The short version of the story is that I had a stalker—an obsessed fan. He harassed me for months, then finally attacked me, was arrested, and locked up. I thought it was over and done with, but I just got word that he's escaped from the loony bin and is probably heading to find me."

"An escaped psycho. This just keeps getting better."

At Michael's sarcastic tone, Diamond frowned at him. "This is hardly my idea of an adventure."

"Why didn't you choose someone else's car to ram off the road?"

The question wasn't really directed at her, she realized. And she understood that this was hardly an ideal situation—especially for this stranger. Still, he didn't have to make it sound as if she had planned this just to make his life miserable.

"You know, I'm really sorry that I panicked, and even sorrier that I hit your car. I understand how *inconvenient* this must be for you, so why don't you just turn around and bring me back to my car before I ruin your day any further?"

He looked at her then. "So that I can have even more guilt to deal with when they find your body?"

Momentarily stunned, Diamond only gaped at him. She certainly didn't appreciate the comment about them finding her body, but she suddenly realized that he'd said something about *even more guilt.* Exactly what did he mean by that?

"What do you mean 'even more guilt'?"

Pause. "Nothing."

"I don't believe you," Diamond went on, pressing the issue. "You wouldn't have said it if you didn't mean it."

He ground out a frustrated sound. "Let's just say, you're not the only one with problems."

"I never said I was."

"Whatever."

Diamond knew she couldn't expect a courteous host given the situation, but she had the distinct feeling that she would be better off out on the road dealing with Clay than sitting in this car with Michael.

"I wasn't kidding when I said you can take me back to my car," she told him.

"It's not gonna happen," he replied bluntly. He blew out a hurried breath. "Look, I'm sorry if I'm not what you expected of a getaway driver, but it's been a long day, you've wrecked my car, and now I have no idea what kind of trouble I may have just gotten myself into by being with you."

"Sorry."

"No, don't apologize. This is the pattern of my life."

"Maybe . . . maybe you'll tell me about it? It helps to get it off your chest."

"No need to depress you, too."

Diamond sat back in her seat. She could only

offer to be there for him, but if he didn't want to talk, she couldn't force him. And she couldn't say that she didn't understand his reservations.

She glanced out at the road as Michael exited I-75 into Naples. "Where are we going?"

"Not too far."

"What does that mean?"

He flashed her a wry grin. "Afraid I'm taking you to the nearest swamp?"

Diamond's lips curled in a sarcastic grin. "I wouldn't be surprised."

Michael actually chuckled. "I guess you picked the wrong car to smash into, didn't you?"

Diamond knew he was joking with her, though it wasn't exactly the kind of joke she wanted to hear right now. Not given the reality she had endured with Clay.

That must have shown on her face, because Michael said, "All right. Maybe that was the wrong thing to say. Relax, I'm taking you to my place."

"Your place?"

"Where else would we go?"

Diamond glanced out the window at the tree-lined street. "No, you're right. That makes sense."

There sure were a lot of trees in Naples, Diamond noted. Different from what she normally saw in the Miami area. She recognized the tall, sprawling oaks from older areas in Miami, like Coral Gables and Coconut Grove. But there were other leafy trees she hadn't seen before, along with bushy palms and thick pines.

"If you did see that crazy guy on the road," Michael said, "I don't think he caught up to us. At least I don't see any car behind us that looks familiar."

"Thank God." Diamond felt somewhat foolish

for how she had reacted. She hoped she hadn't imagined seeing Clay. But given her state of mind, she didn't doubt that was a possibility. She was jumpy and on edge. "I guess I'll hang out at your place for a few hours just to be sure, then go back and get my car."

"I don't want to alarm you, but if you did see that guy out there and he knows you left your car, he could be waiting there for you to return. If he's as nuts as you say he is."

"Oh, darn." A frown played on Diamond's lips. She hadn't thought of that.

"Maybe you're better off having it towed to my place. Or an auto shop, since it will need some work. Whatever, I don't think you're in the best state to make that decision tonight. You seem pretty frazzled. Not that I blame you," he quickly added.

"I guess you're right." Diamond paused as she looked at him. "Are you always this good a judge of character?"

Not always, he thought sourly. But he said, "Comes with the territory."

They fell into silence as Michael made a series of turns, which led him off the main streets and onto a more secluded stretch of road. This was nothing like Miami, Diamond thought, where most of the areas were well developed and filled with apartment complexes or shopping plazas. She had driven through Naples once and wondered how anyone could live in such a sleepy town.

Diamond loved the excitement of Fort Lauderdale and Miami and couldn't imagine living anywhere else. Which was the one thing that really peeved her about Clay's escape. He had forced her to run for her safety, forced her to leave the place she loved, the people she loved. And she had no clue when she would be able to return home.

Minutes later, Michael slowed the car and turned right into a driveway. Diamond hadn't even noticed a driveway was coming up because so many trees surrounded the opening and provided shade throughout the property. In fact, it seemed as if they'd driven into a forest, except for the fact that she could see the small house at the end of the long gravel path.

"This is my humble house," Michael announced as he put the car in park moments later.

Humble it was. It was a modest one-story wood house. While one side of the house seemed to have been newly painted, the other side's paint was chipping badly.

This was . . . country.

Oh, well. Beggars couldn't be choosers, and she was definitely begging.

While Michael opened the door and got out of the car, Diamond lingered behind. He was a cop, and her heart said she could trust him, but suddenly she wondered how smart it was to be going into his place. After all, she'd barely met this man.

But he was keeping her safe from Clay—going out of his way to do so—when he could easily have dumped her on the highway's shoulder to avoid any hassles.

Still, now that she was here, in such a secluded spot, she couldn't help wondering if anyone would remember seeing her on the side of the road with Michael—*should* anything happen. Lord, she hoped so.

Michael walked up to the front door, and Diamond suddenly felt something other than concern as she watched him. She watched him with a growing sense of physical admiration.

For the first time, she allowed herself to *really* look at him. He was tall, at least six feet three from what she could tell. And, quite simply, he was sexy as hell.

He turned then, almost as if he had sensed her staring. Diamond opened the door and stepped out onto the gravel.

"Let me guess," Michael said. "You're second-guessing your decision to jump in my car."

Diamond blew out a slow breath and shrugged nonchalantly. "You can't be this smart simply from being a cop. You studied psychology, right?"

"I was also in the military for five years."

"Any public service you haven't done?"

"I haven't been a firefighter, nor a paramedic. Though I can perform CPR with the best of them."

Was that a hint of a smile Diamond saw on his lips? She couldn't be sure.

She strolled toward him and he said, "It's perfectly normal for you to have some reservations about staying here. You wouldn't be human if you didn't. You wouldn't be smart if you didn't. But, I assure you"—he made a cross sign over his heart— "I will not hurt you."

His words set her mind at ease. It was what she had sensed about him, and she trusted her instincts.

Michael unlocked and opened the front door, then held it open so she could step inside. Inside the foyer, Diamond did a slow turn. The place was small. Quaint. And compared to the exterior, it was in much better shape. Diamond got the impression Michael had recently been doing work on the interior, because everything looked so new.

The hardwood floor sparkled. The eggshell-white walls didn't have a single mark. Even the contemporary sofa and matching love seat in the nearby living room looked like they'd just come off a showroom floor.

"This place has three bedrooms, but I'm using one as a workroom. The other ... well, it's off-limits."

Diamond simply nodded, though she wanted to ask why he would have a room that was off-limits. It wasn't so much that it was off-limits that made her curious, but the way he said it. She had so many questions where he was concerned. Questions she knew she had no business asking.

Instead, she asked, "Are you doing renovations?"

"Yes."

Diamond glanced around. "If you've done all this work I see here, then I'm very impressed."

"It's peaceful here, and I have a lot of time on my hands."

Diamond took a few steps toward the living room, then stopped. "My goodness. I didn't even think of this. Do you have a wife or girlfriend?" No woman had greeted him, but perhaps she was at work. "I don't want to put you in a bad situation."

"This already is a ..." Michael paused, clearly considering his words. "An *interesting* situation. But no, I don't have a wife or girlfriend."

"That's good. I mean, considering."

"I know what you mean."

There was a moment of silence; then Michael said, "I need to check on something. I'll be back in a little while."

"Right. Of course."

"Make yourself at home. There's juice in the fridge. Probably not much to munch on, though."

Diamond nodded, then watched as Michael headed off down the hallway.

Her gaze lingered on his body, and an unexpected shiver snaked down her spine. He was definitely easy on the eyes. Despite her distraught state after she'd run into his car, she had not failed to notice the man's purely masculine appeal.

His body was long and lean and proportionately muscular, from what she could tell within his loose-fitting jeans. And there was no denying that Michael was gorgeous. Not just in the traditional way, though his face was very pleasant to look at. But there was an aura about him that oozed strength and power.

And she had to admit, the man sure did have one hell of a sexy walk. It was the kind of walk that would command attention when he entered a room.

Michael could easily fit any woman's fantasy of an African god. She wondered if his face lit up when he smiled.

He had to be at least thirty. He was strong, seemingly healthy. Clearly, he wasn't a bum. And Diamond knew firsthand how some women lost their heads over a man in uniform, so if he was a cop, why would he still be single?

Surely he could have his share of women . . .

Maybe that's it, Diamond thought sourly. Despite his age, Michael simply didn't want to settle down. He was the type of man who enjoyed his single life—enjoyed bedding woman after woman without any commitment.

Diamond rose to her feet. Slowly, she strolled in the same direction Michael had just gone. She wasn't quite sure what she was looking for, other than something that would tell her more about Michael. He had a mysterious quality, and Diamond couldn't help it—she was drawn to intrigue like a moth was drawn to a flame.

Perhaps that was why she had gone into her chosen field of work. From the time she had studied journalism, she had always been intrigued by the dynamics of male-female relationships. And she seemed to give pretty good advice in both her newspaper column and on her radio show—not that she had been able to get her own love life together.

She sighed, thinking of that sad fact. Her last boyfriend had proven to her that she absolutely couldn't make a decent choice when it came to men. Like Michael, Paul was a cop—someone she had believed she could trust.

Diamond could not have been more wrong. Paul had been almost as bad as Clay. Worse, even. Sure, she had understood his concern for her safety as a public figure, but to try and scare her into quitting by "stalking" her, even if he meant her no harm, was as low as someone could go. She had a right to make decisions for herself, whether he liked them or not.

In hindsight, Diamond knew she had rushed into a relationship with Paul. At the time, she had been on the rebound from Tyrone—the man she had truly been in love with. However, Tyrone had devastated her by cheating on her with *his* ex, and she had desperately needed someone to take away her pain—even if she now regretted her actions.

After Tyrone, Diamond had come to the sad realization that you simply couldn't trust a man with all your heart. That's why she had run head-

long into a relationship with Paul, caring only
about companionship and her physical needs, not
about building a foundation for a lasting relationship.

But whatever the future held for her, she would
not make the same mistakes. No more rushing into
a relationship based on physical attraction without
getting to know a man first.

Not that she was even thinking about a relationship these days. Her cousin Tara had unexpectedly
found love after a horrible heartbreak, and Diamond was happy for her, but Diamond didn't have
the same hopes for herself. She was content to
concentrate on her work at the radio station.
Maybe she would do a few more public appearances, make sure to keep her schedule extremely
busy so she would have no time to think of anything
else.

Realizing that she had stopped in the hallway
with her thoughts, Diamond continued walking.
But she paused again. Did she hear voices coming
from the first room?

Diamond crept up to the door and pressed her
ear against it. She could clearly hear the voice of
a woman coming from what she realized must be
the answering machine.

". . . sorry. Look, I didn't mean to deceive you—
it's just that . . . you know how much I worry about
you, and you've already taken so much time for
yourself. Please, call me. I don't want this to come
between us."

For a long moment, Diamond stood there, listening for more. A weird tingling spread through
her body, the kind that came with disappointment.
So, there was a woman after all. Of course. Dia-

mond shouldn't be disappointed, but for some reason, she was.

Hearing the shuffling of feet, Diamond hurried away from the door and back to the living room. As she plopped down on the sofa, she knew what bothered her. Not that Michael was involved with someone—of course he would be—but the fact that he had lied about it. Why had he bothered to make her believe he wasn't involved with anyone?

Why did it matter to her either way?

Because she'd had a very stressful couple of days, and was irrationally emotional over things that shouldn't matter.

This was a bad idea for more than one reason. For one thing, she didn't need anything else to make her emotional right now, rationally provoked or not. And most importantly, she certainly didn't need to get caught up in someone else's relationship. His girlfriend—whoever she was—would not be thrilled to learn that Diamond was staying at her boyfriend's place. And considering she wasn't making a play for Michael, why bother with the headache?

Diamond had made her decision. When Michael came out of the bedroom, she would ask him to give her a ride back to her car so she could be on her way.

She sat waiting as the minutes ticked by. Michael didn't return to the living room.

Finally, Diamond jumped to her feet. She headed down the hallway and rapped on the bedroom door she had stood outside of a short time earlier.

No answer.

Frowning, Diamond knocked again. That's when she heard the sound of running water.

Michael was showering.

Diamond wandered farther down the hall, following the sound. She stopped outside the bathroom door and rested against the wall. Right inside this room, Michael was naked.

Why did that thought set her pulse racing?

As much as she had tried to keep herself from acknowledging the thought in a conscious way, as she stood outside the bathroom, she could no longer deny the truth. Michael wasn't just attractive—he was her kind of attractive. The kind of man who could, if she was willing, tempt her into one night of passion she would never forget.

The thought was completely inappropriate, of course. Not only that, but hadn't she told herself that she needed to change her ways? No more thinking with her libido, as it were. She needed to take time to get to know a man before thinking of dating him, much less thinking of sleeping with him. Her mistake with Paul would always haunt her.

Still, she wasn't dead, and it was impossible not to notice that Michael was one gorgeous specimen of a man.

Diamond lingered outside the bathroom door a moment longer. *What does he look like completely naked?*

"My goodness," she said, heaving herself off the wall with both hands. What was she doing, standing out here, acting like a common pervert? She had seen enough men naked before that she didn't have to stand here, letting her imagination run wild with thoughts that didn't make sense, considering she had met Michael only hours before.

Ashamed of herself, Diamond scurried back to the living room. Her mind was made up. When

Michael got out of the shower, she would tell him her decision.

She was going to leave—tonight. And the sooner the better.

CHAPTER THREE

But when Michael entered the living room nearly an hour after disappearing, Diamond didn't say a thing. Suddenly, the words she had planned to say would not roll off her tongue.

She hadn't known what to expect, but she certainly hadn't expected to see Michael clad only in a pair of cutoff denim shorts.

Dear Lord. The man was practically naked. And he looked even better than what she had imagined a short while earlier.

Diamond's eyes perused him from head to toe. The man was definitely blessed in the physique department. His shoulders were broad and beautifully sculpted. He had a firm body, shapely pecs and biceps, and while it was obvious he worked out, he wasn't too bulky, like some men who routinely worked out. His skin was a beautiful medium brown.

There was a sprinkling of black hair on Michael's chest that grew moderately thicker as it went lower. The hair didn't obscure his belly button, which,

Diamond saw with pleasure, was an "inny." She had a thing for belly buttons.

But she also had a thing for powerful thighs, which Michael most definitely possessed. If she didn't know any better, she would say he had come out here barely dressed and showing off his amazing body so that he could seduce her.

Diamond raised her gaze to meet Michael's. A chill hit her like a slap in the face. One look at his deadpan expression and she knew she had gone off into la-la land without cause. It was obvious that Michael had no desire to seduce her.

"Hey." Diamond's voice croaked.

"Sorry I took so long," Michael said. "I had to make a couple phone calls, grab a shower."

"Yes, I see." Diamond swallowed.

"Are you hungry?"

Diamond couldn't lie. "I am."

"You probably discovered that I don't have anything decent in the fridge."

She flashed a sheepish smile. "Right again."

"Sorry about that. Since I live here alone, I usually pick up food a little at a time. Or when I'm hungry. In any case, I don't really feel like going out to grab a bite tonight, but we can order some food."

"Actually . . ."

Michael raised an eyebrow as he looked at her.

"I was thinking you could take me back to get my car." Her voice was timid, knowing she was putting him out of his way. He had a life that he had been living before she fell into his world. "I really thank you for your hospitality, but I should probably be on my way."

"You know where you're going?"

"I'll find a place. Which, of course, is my problem, not yours."

"Ouch."

"Sorry. I didn't mean that to come off as gruff. It's just that I know this is an awkward situation for you, and I don't want to make it worse with your girlfriend showing up . . ."

"My girlfriend?"

Diamond glanced away, then back at him. "Don't be mad, but I was heading down the hall—looking for the bathroom—and I heard what must have been your answering machine. A woman saying she was sorry for something. I quickly stepped away, but I heard enough to know . . . to know that I have to leave. You two are already fighting, and my being here is only going to make things worse, which you don't need. Nor deserve."

"You've got it all figured out."

"I'm a woman. I know how I'd feel if my man were to bring home some female he had met on the side of the road. Besides, I hear this kind of story all too often on my radio show—a situation that starts out fairly harmlessly is blown out of proportion by a partner who's too jealous or insecure. I'm not trying to say your girlfriend's insecure . . . Look, there's no point in taking the risk that she'll have a problem with this when I can just leave."

Michael crossed his arms over his strong chest. "So you give people advice?"

"I'm not a certified shrink or anything, but yes, I offer my opinion. Based on my own experiences and perceptions."

Michael merely nodded, then turned and walked to the large living room window.

The guy was cute, but weird. A brooding type,

Diamond realized, which only made her wonder what he was all about.

Michael slowly turned. "I'll leave it up to you what you want to order."

Diamond stared at him for a few seconds before speaking. "What does that mean? You . . . you're completely ignoring what I had to say?"

"Of course I'll take you to get your car."

"Good."

"In the morning."

Diamond's eyes bulged as she stared at him. "What?"

"When I know you've rested, had something to eat. Had some time to think about your situation."

"Michael—"

"If this guy's really after you, and is really as dangerous as you say, then you shouldn't go off on your own without police involvement."

"Huh. Like the cops were able to help before."

"You're better off with them on your side than going it alone."

"I'm better off in Seattle."

Michael's eyebrows shot up. "You're planning on driving to Seattle?"

Diamond waved a dismissive hand. "No. That was a lame attempt at humor."

"Oh. My bad."

"The point is, the farther away from Clay I can get, the better. He won't look for me if I'm in some remote place."

"This place is pretty remote."

Diamond's eyes flew to Michael's in shock. Was she mistaken, or did she also see a measure of shock in his eyes? Yet that didn't make sense, since the words had come from his mouth.

"I'm just trying to say," he went on, "that you

don't have to run off before you've had some time to think. There's no way Clay would find you here. So, you don't have to worry about that.''

''I don't know—''

Before Diamond could get her words out, Michael turned and padded out of the living room. She gaped after him.

Great, she thought, rolling her eyes heavenward. How dare the man just walk away!

Moments later, however, he returned. This time, he carried a telephone book. *Okay, so he went to get the phone book*, Diamond thought, feeling better. He hadn't simply dismissed her.

Approaching her where she sat on the sofa, Michael passed the phone book to her. ''Whatever you want to eat is fine with me. Even if you want anchovies on a pizza.''

Diamond couldn't help giggling. ''Anchovies?'' she asked, making sure she had heard correctly. She had never known anyone who liked anchovies.

''Why not?''

''Because they're awful! They ruin a pizza.''

Michael merely shrugged. ''If you don't want them, don't order them. Doesn't matter to me. Whatever you order, let me know what it costs. I'll pay for it.''

Sensing Michael would be the type to insist on paying if she offered, Diamond gave a brief nod. But she certainly would not make him pay for the meal. After all, he was putting her up for the night. The least she could do was pay for any food.

''Chinese okay?'' she asked.

''Whatever you want.''

''Wow, you're easy.''

For the first time, Michael flashed a smile, albeit

a small one. Then he turned and headed out of
the room once again.

Diamond couldn't help frowning. There was
something definitely strange about Michael, something . . .

Sad?

As the word hit her, it shocked her. But it also
resonated with truth.

Yes, sad. There was an aura of sadness around
Michael. She suddenly felt it so deeply and pro-
foundly that she wondered how she hadn't noticed
it before.

What had happened to him? Why had he taken
a leave of absence from the force?

What had led him to living in a secluded house
in Naples?

It had been a pure stroke of luck.

Happening to see Diamond on the highway as
he was heading to Miami to find her—Clay
couldn't have asked for better luck.

She had been in some type of fender bender
and was out of her car, which is why he'd been
able to identify her easily. His mouth hanging open
in shock, Clay had slowed down, then searched for
a spot to turn around on the highway.

That's when she must have seen him, because
she'd run to that guy's car like a spooked horse.

Diamond didn't give him enough credit, Clay
thought with annoyance. That had been the problem right from the beginning. When was she going
to learn that she couldn't run from him forever?

He knew she wanted to be with him, so why was
she bothering to play her games? Her games made
him angry.

Clay slowed down on the stretch of I-75, glancing at Diamond's car on the shoulder. She hadn't been back for it. He had been cruising back and forth on the highway for hours, hoping she would return. He would have to turn around at the nearest exit and double back.

His mind replayed the first moment he had seen her on the highway—he had been elated and nervous at the same time. It had been so long . . . But the elation had soon turned to anger when he saw her getting into the car with that guy. Anger that the stupid whore was betraying him again.

All the time he had been away, he hadn't stopped thinking of her. He had dreamed of the way it would be when they reunited, how it would feel to hold her in his arms again.

He had clung to the belief that she missed him as much as he missed her. That thought had gotten him through all those nights in that horrible place.

So what was she doing with that other guy? Was this guy merely helping her because her car had broken down?

Clay had tried to turn around in time to follow them, but the jerk driving the car had sped up so fast that it was impossible for him to catch up to them. For the next few hours, he had driven back and forth on the highway, hoping Diamond would return for what had to be her car.

But she hadn't returned.

Well, not yet.

But she would. She had to. And when she did, Clay would be waiting.

CHAPTER FOUR

"Diamond!" Tara exclaimed. She sounded exasperated and relieved at the same time. "Where are you?"

Hearing her cousin's voice, Diamond couldn't help smiling. She and Tara were as close as sisters. In fact, Diamond had always felt closer to Tara than she had to her sister, Marcia. Maybe that's because Marcia was ten years older, so they had never gone through similar life experiences at the same time. And after college, Marcia had moved to New Orleans and gotten married.

Diamond said, "Don't panic, Tara. I'm okay."

"Where are you?" Tara repeated firmly.

"I'm in Naples."

"Naples?" Tara paused, clearly letting that sink in. "What on earth are you doing in Naples?"

"It's a long story."

"Are you staying with someone or are you in a hotel?"

"I—I had a weird day, one I'll tell you about

later ." Diamond didn't want to get into everything right now. "All that matters is I'm safe."

Tara groaned. "Diamond, we've been so worried. Your call scared me half out of my mind."

"I'm fine."

"For now. Clay is out there. You're obviously scared enough to be running."

"I figure if I lie low for a while, he'll go away." But Diamond was lying. She did not believe that Clay would just go away. Yet she didn't want her cousin to worry.

"I don't like this," Tara said. "You out there alone. Come back home and we'll make sure you're safe. If Clay tries anything here, he won't get away with it."

Diamond frowned. If only she could be so sure. But where Clay was concerned, Diamond had no clue what he might do. How desperate he was. She only knew that he was extremely resourceful.

And extremely obsessed with her.

Besides, she didn't want Clay to try *anything*. It had been bad enough the first time, so she didn't want to be anyplace where she might be bait.

"I've had car trouble," Diamond told her cousin. "I can't head back right now, regardless."

"Tell me where you are and we'll come get you."

By "we," Tara meant her and her husband of five weeks, Darren Burkeen. Darren had come into Tara's life unexpectedly, after her fiancé had broken their engagement by getting engaged to someone else. Tara, a consummate planner, had naturally been devastated by the demise of her five-year relationship. And when Darren had come into her life, professing his instant love for her, she had done her best to push him away, unable to believe in something as obscure as love at first sight. But over time, Darren had proven to her with romance and old-fashioned courting that he truly was in love with her, and now the two were happily married.

"Aren't you still honeymooning?" Diamond asked, forcing a smile into her voice. "You and Darren have other things to worry about besides me."

There was a pause, then, "You're not serious, are you?"

"Kind of."

"I can't believe you said that. How could we not be worried about you?"

"I know . . . Sorry. I'm just trying to let you know in my own silly way that I'm fine. There's really no need for you and Darren to worry."

"Well, we are."

"Please try not to."

Tara sighed. "I'll try. At least your telephone call has made me feel better."

"And I'll stay in touch with you as much as you need me to until I get back to Miami. Which really shouldn't be long. Like I said, I think Clay will disappear once he doesn't find me. Better yet, maybe the police will spot him and take him in."

"You sound pretty confident." Tara spoke cautiously.

"I am," Diamond assured her. "Oh, and can you do me a favor and call my parents to let them know I'm all right?"

"I'm sure they'll want to hear from you personally."

"You know my mother. She'll have heart failure, no matter what I tell her."

"And if she hears my voice instead of yours, she'll really panic."

Diamond bit her inner cheek. She wasn't ready to call her parents, because she didn't have any answers for them. But Tara was right. They would worry a lot more if she had Tara call them on her behalf.

"You're right. I'll give them a call."

"Is there a number where I can reach you?" Tara asked.

"My cell."

Tara sighed again. Diamond knew she was worried, and she loved her for that. "All right. Diamond, I really hope you're okay."

"I am."

"You'd tell me if you weren't, right?"

"Of course I would. In fact, I'm not as stressed out as I was when I called you. I'm away from Miami, and there's no way Clay can know where I am. And don't worry—I'm going to stay in touch with the police, because I want to know when they find Clay. Then I can head back home without any worries."

"Okay." Tara sounded a little more upbeat. "I guess that makes sense. I can't believe Clay escaped."

"Neither can I. Honestly, how could something like this happen?"

"That's a great question, but it does happen— all too often."

"I know." Diamond drew in a deep breath, but it didn't calm her. "Anyway, I'm sure this will all be over sooner rather than later."

"I'm praying that's the case."

"Thanks. I'll talk to you later."

"Okay. 'Bye."

Diamond disconnected her cell phone. Though she'd told Tara she could be reached her via her cell, she didn't know how much longer that would remain true. The battery was running low, and her charger was in her car.

And of course, her car was nowhere near here.

At least anyone calling her would get her voice mail. Not that she expected that to make any of her family members feel better, but it was the only option for the time being.

Diamond was glad to have reached her parents' voice mail when she called them. She left an upbeat message for them so they wouldn't worry, assuring her mother and father that she was okay, and that she would be in touch soon. It was much more preferable to leave a message than to answer a bunch of questions.

Diamond's thoughts wandered to Michael. Why had he retired to his room and left her out here alone for so long? Sure, it had to be odd having a stranger in your living room. Still, did he plan on leaving her on her own for the rest of the evening? Especially since when he'd left, he had told her to order food.

Perhaps he had heard her speaking on the phone and was simply giving her some privacy. She hoped that was the case.

Her thoughts were interrupted by the sound of knocking at the door. Diamond jumped up from the sofa, grabbing her purse as she did. Seconds later, she was at the front door.

"Hi." She smiled at the deliveryman as she took the pizza box from him. After going back and forth on the issue of what they would eat, she'd finally decided on a pizza. No one could mess up a pizza. Besides, it was one of her favorite foods.

"Thanks so much," Diamond told the man. The pizza smelled delicious. Turning, she placed the box on a small table in the foyer, then reached into her purse. She passed the man some cash, which included a generous tip, then closed the door behind him.

Once again she picked up the pizza box. She took a few steps forward, then to the right, into the kitchen and dining area. "Michael," she called. "Dinner's here."

Diamond placed the pizza on the kitchen counter. She spent the next several seconds opening various cupboards, searching for plates. She found some, brought two to the table, then tore off some sheets of paper towels to use as napkins.

She turned—and gave a gasp of shock when she saw Michael standing only a few feet behind her. Yes, she had called him, but she hadn't even heard him come into the room. The man was as quiet as a cat.

"Didn't mean to scare you," he said simply.

At least now he was wearing a T-shirt, though her mind easily conjured up the image of what he had looked like without one.

"I ordered pizza," Diamond told him, speaking with a calmness that surprised her, considering her pounding heart. Why did she feel so flustered?

Clay, of course. She was on edge because of him.

"It smells good." Michael walked to the pizza box and lifted the cover.

"No anchovies." Diamond smiled.

Michael carried the box to the table. "I'm not an anchovies fan. Just not a fussy eater."

Diamond pulled out a chair and sat. "I guess that's a good way to be. Sometimes I'm a little too picky. In any case, I hope you don't mind that I didn't get any meat toppings.''

"It's all good.''

Michael reached for a slice, and Diamond followed his example. They ate in silence for several minutes.

"Oh.'' Diamond suddenly stood. "I forgot to get something to drink.'' She walked to the fridge and opened it. Scanning the contents, she saw only orange juice and cola. "What do you want?'' she asked Michael without turning. "Juice or soda?''

"Juice is good.''

Diamond withdrew the carton from the fridge. She found two glasses in a cupboard and filled them both with juice. Then she rejoined Michael at the table.

"Thanks,'' he said, taking the glass from her before she could place it on the table. He took a liberal sip.

"So,'' Diamond began, "you live out here alone?''

"Yes.''

"What do you do out here? This place seems so . . . isolated from the world.''

"That's the way I like it.''

Diamond's eyebrows shot up. The man was a mystery, all right. "I've got to tell you, that's pretty hard for me to understand.'' Diamond chuckled. "I guess I'm a bit of a social butterfly. I like busy places, lots of malls. A movie theater around every corner.''

"Where do you live?''

"Coral Gables.''

Michael nodded. "There's a lot of action for you there, no doubt.''

"Yeah, but mostly I'm too busy to enjoy it. I work

a lot. And I do a lot of public appearances and fund-raisers for various charities.''

"Work related?"

Diamond nodded as she took a bite of her pizza.

Michael stretched out in his chair. "Some people like a lot of action. Me, I'm quite happy where I am. I don't miss it at all."

"So you haven't always lived here?"

"No. I was a cop in Fort Lauderdale."

Diamond's eyes lit up. "Wow. Fort Lauderdale. And now you're living *here?*"

"People change."

"Yeah, but that's quite a change." And she couldn't help wondering why. So she asked. "Why would you leave the force and move to Naples?"

"You ask a lot of questions."

Diamond finished chewing, then washed her pizza down with a swig of orange juice. "I guess I'm used to asking a lot of questions."

Michael didn't say anything, and Diamond soon realized that he had no plans to fill in the blanks for her. She suddenly felt like she was prying, rather than simply trying to make conversation.

She ate another slice of pizza, waiting for Michael to initiate the next topic, but he didn't. Finally, she said, "I appreciate you taking me in like this. I know this hasn't exactly been easy for you. I'm a stranger, practically invading your space. And you're a guy who clearly values his privacy."

"It's no problem. Like I told you, I wouldn't want to leave you in a bad situation. One night out of my life isn't going to kill me."

"Well, thanks again."

"There's not much to do here, but I do have some movies if you want to pass the time."

Diamond nodded. She had a feeling she would

need to do something to avoid dying of boredom. "Yeah, that would be cool."

"Like I said, two rooms are out of commission. But I'll let you sleep in my room and I'll take the sofa."

"Oh, that's not necessary. The sofa will be fine for me."

"I insist. Besides, sometimes I like to catch a late movie or something on TV, so I won't mind being in the living room."

"If it works better for you that way, sure."

"I'll survive for one night. Whenever you're ready, let me know and I'll give you a shirt to sleep in."

One night. As Diamond watched Michael rise from the table and bring his dirty plate to the sink, she realized just how bizarre this situation was. There was something completely odd about Michael, even though she felt she could trust him.

Getting him to talk was like pulling teeth. If they watched a movie together, would he even say a word to her?

Michael turned to her. "I'm going to head back to my room to continue doing some work."

"Sure." But she wanted to ask, *What kind of work?* After all, he was on leave from the force.

Diamond's gaze followed Michael as he left the kitchen. Once he was out of sight, she leaned back in her chair and groaned. She had a feeling this was going to be the longest night of her life.

CHAPTER FIVE

Michael dropped onto the bed when he entered his bedroom. As he lay back, a long breath oozed out of his lungs.

His insides felt all twisted and out of whack. Part of him felt bad for being the most unsociable host possible, while another part of him wanted to stay hidden until it was time to take Diamond back to get her car.

So why not just take her back to her car now, like she asked you to?

As appealing as that idea was, it was something he wouldn't do. He didn't doubt that Diamond was in real trouble, and the last thing he wanted to do was put her in a bad situation.

If only it hadn't been today that she had smashed into him, today that she had jumped into his car. His mind was on the anniversary that had just passed—the very anniversary Kelly had not wanted him to face alone.

But he had—the way he always would. Debra wasn't at his side to tell him that everything would be all right, which maybe was a blessing after all. He wouldn't believe her words of comfort, even if she were here. How could everything be all right, when Ashley was gone?

It seemed like both a lifetime and only yesterday since he had last held his beautiful little girl. In reality, it had been a year. The most painful year of his life.

When Michael had married Debra, he had been naive enough to believe in "till death do us part" and "happily ever after." He had been naive enough to believe that a couple in love could have a child that wouldn't die. But he had been wrong on both counts.

It hadn't taken Debra long to leave him after Ashley's death. Her initial hysteria over Ashley's death had quickly turned to blame. Michael had been the one home with his daughter at the time she had died. Without warning, she had stopped breathing. By the time Michael had noticed, it had been too late.

He squeezed his eyes shut against the horrible memory. When he had found his daughter's still body in her crib . . . God, how he had been frantic. He had barely kept his head together to administer CPR. Not that it had done any good.

A chill settled in his heart, the chill that always came with the memory. And like so many other times, Michael thought of the one thing that would make the memory go away.

Numb him, actually. Make him forget the pain. Alcohol.

He sucked in a sharp breath. Held it. Let the craving pass. He didn't try and fool himself with the belief that one drink was all he needed. At least not anymore. He had done just that in the past, but one drink had always led to two, and suddenly he was waking up the next morning with a killer hangover and no knowledge of what had happened for several hours.

He wasn't proud of how he'd handled his grief, but it had been the only thing he could do in the beginning to get past those very dark days. He'd longed for Debra to hold him, cry with him, promise him that everything would be all right.

Tell him that she forgave him.

But Debra hadn't been there.

Kelly had assured him that Ashley's death wasn't his fault. The doctor had also told him the same thing. In his heart, he knew it was true. Babies died of sudden infant death syndrome for no apparent reason. He had tried to comfort himself with the thought that at least he had been blessed with little Ashley for seven months, but the thought always fell short of soothing his broken heart.

As hard as it had been to deal with his pain alone, Debra had done him a favor. Her leaving had crushed the last of his dreams, and now he knew not to be so foolish as to believe in a happily ever after again. His parents hadn't found it; what had ever made him think he would?

He was alone, and the move to Naples had been just what he needed. He needed to be physically alone to match his emotional state. If only he could figure out a job to do at home, everything would be perfect.

"I'm so worried about you," he heard Kelly say. "You're wasting away out there . . ."

Michael sat up abruptly. He didn't like the direction of his thoughts. The past was the past; he wanted to leave it there.

Needed to leave it there.

At least for the time being, because he had a guest to entertain. And perhaps this guest could truly help take his mind off yesterday's anniversary that he wished he could forget.

Lying back once more, Michael groaned, suddenly angry at himself for that thought. The anniversary of his daughter's death was something he should never, ever forget. And did he want even a moment's reprieve from his pain? With the pain was the proof that his daughter had lived. If he didn't have his pain, what would he have?

Ashley was dead. What right did he have to go on?

Michael had shared his feelings with Kelly once, and she'd told him that he would feel differently in time. So far, he didn't—and as crazy as it sounded, he wasn't altogether sure that he wanted to.

And even if he did want a distraction from his pain, did he want it in the form of the beautiful, spunky woman a room away?

Michael rolled onto his side. He was disturbed by Diamond more than he cared to admit. Something about her knocked his equilibrium off kilter. Was it her spunk, her endless curiosity, at a time when he wanted to be alone to grieve? Or was it something else?

He didn't know, but something stirred inside him whenever he looked at her. Something that made him feel much more at ease staying away from her.

"Tomorrow," he told himself. "She'll be gone tomorrow."

There was no reason to act as if she were some permanent fixture in his life. And it would be the height of ignorance to leave her alone to entertain herself all night.

After all, she didn't know what he was going through.

A couple of movies. How hard could that be?

Michael slowly sat up, then got to his feet. He headed for the living room, determined to be social.

Diamond's lips curled in a smile as Michael walked into the living room. It was such a simple thing, but it reminded him of all that he had missed out on in the past year.

Reminded him that he was alone.

The television was on, and the volume was low. Diamond said, "I thought maybe you'd dozed off. I hope I didn't wake you."

"No. I was just . . ." *Trying my best to stay away from you.* "It doesn't matter. What matters is that for the rest of the evening, you will have my attention. Now, you said you might want to watch a movie?"

"Sure."

Michael walked over to his entertainment center and opened one of the doors. "I have a ton of movies. Take your pick." The movies had been his link to the real world over the past several months. Though he hadn't been interested in communicating with anyone, watching movies had kept him from feeling completely isolated.

Diamond was suddenly at his side. "Wow. You have quite the collection."

"VHS and DVDs."

Diamond faced him. "Do you feel in the mood for anything in particular?"

"Something funny." Lord knew, he didn't want to watch anything that might heighten the emotions of yesterday's anniversary, not with Diamond here.

"A comedy." Diamond bent to peruse the titles. "Sure."

Two movies later, it was a few minutes after eleven P.M. Diamond, who was resting her head on the armrest, yawned. She couldn't keep her eyes open much longer.

"You sleeping?" Michael asked.

"No . . . but I'm tired."

"You should have told me."

Diamond sat up, smiling. "I'll survive."

"I changed the sheets, so whenever you're ready to go to bed . . ."

"In that case." Diamond stood.

"Let me grab you a T-shirt."

Michael headed out of the living room, and Diamond followed him. He led her to the first bedroom on the right and opened the door.

As Diamond followed him into the room, she suddenly felt weird. When was the last time she had gone into a man's bedroom when she hadn't been about to make love to him?

She couldn't remember.

"Like I said, the sheets are clean." Michael strolled to the dresser. He dug out a shirt and held it out to her. "Here's a shirt. Is there anything else you need?"

"A toothbrush?"

"I'll see if I can find you one."

Michael moved to step past her, but she also

stepped in the same direction in an attempt to move out of his way. Their bodies collided.

Diamond stumbled, and Michael reached out to steady her.

"Sorry," she said. She looked into his eyes, which were dark and intense. And she couldn't help noticing how strong his hands were on her arms.

Releasing her, he glanced away. So did Diamond. She suddenly felt more awkward than she figured normal for this situation.

"I'll look for a toothbrush."

"Right."

Michael closed the door behind him on the way out. Blowing out a breath, Diamond sauntered toward the bed. She easily slipped her black cotton dress over her head, then got into Michael's T-shirt. Michael was a very tall man, and the T-shirt reached her almost to her knees.

She took a step closer to the bed. Then stopped. Michael's bed. She couldn't help wondering if he shared it with a woman—or several.

Not that it should matter.

If there was a woman, Diamond didn't think she spent much time here—except, perhaps, in this bedroom. The place lacked a woman's touch. And glancing around, Diamond didn't see any photos of a woman. No photos of anyone, for that matter.

"Goodness, Diamond, stop playing amateur detective." Michael's private life was none of her business.

She moved to the side of the bed and yanked down the top cover. At the sound of the knock on the door, she jumped, startled. Regaining her composure, she called, "Come in."

The door slowly opened, but Michael didn't

enter. He stood in the door's frame, a toothbrush in hand.

For several seconds, he didn't speak. Instead, his eyes perused her body from head to toe, leaving a path of heat over every part they touched.

Diamond's breath caught in her throat. Was she mistaken, or was he checking her out?

"Um . . ." Diamond was surprised to find her voice was hoarse. "You found a toothbrush?"

Michael quickly looked away, as if embarrassed to be caught staring. "Yeah. Here it is."

Still, he didn't walk into the room. Diamond got the impression he was afraid to.

Why?

She made her way to him and took the toothbrush he offered. "Thanks."

"Towels are in the linen closet right outside the bathroom."

"Great."

There was a pause as Michael once again met her gaze head-on. "Good night."

"See you in the morning."

The next morning, Diamond awoke suddenly. A sense of panic filling her, her eyes popped open. In that first instant from slumber to wakefulness, she didn't know where she was.

It took only a couple more seconds for her memory to kick in. She was in Michael's bed.

Quickly, she sat up, twisting around to look for a clock. She found one high on the wall behind the bed. Not the most convenient spot for a clock, she thought. She eased forward so she could get a good look.

Her heart slammed against her rib cage when she saw the time. It was minutes to eleven!

Good grief, where had the time gone? She must have been more tired than she'd realized. Which made sense. Yesterday had been a long and emotionally draining day.

Even though several aged oaks provided shade in the yard, rays of sunlight still made their way into Michael's bedroom. It was almost alarming to hear no sounds—no cars, no people outside. It truly felt as if Diamond had gone to another country.

Throwing off the covers, she swung her feet over the side of the bed. She listened for sounds in the house but heard only birds chirping outside. Such a simple pleasure, but when was the last time she had enjoyed it? She couldn't help smiling.

She turned her attention back to the house. Still, she heard nothing. Given the hour, she didn't think Michael could still be sleeping. Or could he?

Diamond wanted to take a shower, but she didn't have any fresh clothes or underwear to change into. Her best bet was to get back to her car, then hit the road. It was early, but she was sure a hotel out there would let her check in.

Diamond slipped her panties on, then her dress. The hardwood floor was cool beneath her feet as she padded across it to the bedroom door.

Slowly, Diamond opened the door. Again, she listened for sound. Still not hearing anything, she made her way down the hallway to the bathroom.

One look in the mirror nearly gave her heart failure. She wore her auburn-colored hair in a short slicked-back 'do, so it still looked fairly good. But not until this moment did she realize just how unattractive she looked without a stitch of makeup.

She needed to get back to her car—and fast.

She washed her face and brushed her teeth, then went to the living room.

Michael wasn't there, which surprised her. Here she had thought that perhaps he was still sleeping, but he was already up and out of the house.

Diamond made her way to the front door and opened it. Michael's car was parked out front. Clearly, he couldn't be far. But where?

Slowly, his form appeared, rising from behind the back of his car. He had been bending down, and Diamond didn't have to consult a psychic to figure out what he had been looking at.

The car's damage.

Diamond ducked back into the house to slip into her shoes before making her way outside. "How bad is it?" she asked as she approached him.

"Bad enough that I'll have to take it in. But not as bad as I'd initially thought. It might cost little more than the deductible to repair."

"I am sorry," Diamond told him. "You believe that, don't you?"

He nodded as he stole another glance at his bumper.

Diamond crossed her arms over her chest. "What do we do now? I know you need my insurance info, but do we also need a police report?"

"Actually . . ." Michael faced her. "If I get a reasonable quote, would you be all right with paying me out of pocket? I mean, if it's not more than a few hundred bucks to fix, why have a mark against you with your insurance company?"

Diamond smiled. "That's really nice of you, Michael. Yes, I'd prefer that."

"Doesn't matter to me." He paused. "Looks like you're ready to go."

"It's the morning." She spoke cheerfully. "I'm well rested, and look—my hands aren't shaking. I may as well get my car and be on my way."

"I was going to make some breakfast."

"Oh, no. Please don't. I've already put you out. Unless you're hungry. But if not, maybe we can head to get my car now?"

"You sure you don't want to eat anything?"

"Yes."

Michael was silent as he regarded her, and Diamond almost got the feeling that he was going to tell her he wasn't quite ready for her to leave. But that was ridiculous—wasn't it?

Instead, he said, "I wish we could have met under different circumstances."

He did? Diamond's stomach suddenly tensed. Was Michael simply being nice, or did his words carry a heavier meaning?

"This has been a bad few days for me. I haven't been in the best mood."

"And our accident couldn't have made things any better for you. Honestly, Michael, you don't need to feel bad for anything. I'm the one who feels bad. I just appreciate your hospitality in taking me in when I clearly needed someone."

"You know where you're heading?"

"Yeah," Diamond lied. "I was thinking I would head to New Orleans. I have a sister there whom I haven't seen in a while. I can hang out at her place for a week or so. Hopefully the cops will catch Clay in the meantime."

"Hopefully."

"It really sucks when you feel your life is out of your control. That's how I feel now. Not sure of anything anymore."

"Don't I know it." Michael rounded the car toward his front door. "Let me get my car keys."

Diamond watched him disappear, thinking that in an odd way, she would miss him. He had been what she'd needed at the time—someone with a level head to keep her from danger—and she was truly grateful for that. She wondered if he would take offense to her asking for his phone number.

A smile crept onto her face. They would have to be in touch. He still had to tell her how much damage she had done to his car.

Michael returned a minute later, and they got in his car and started off. The first several minutes of the trip passed in silence, but once they hit I-75, Diamond spoke. "Do you want to call me when you've gotten an estimate for the damage on your car, or shall I call you?"

"I'll call you," Michael replied simply.

Diamond merely nodded. "Do you want my insurance information?"

"Nah. I trust you."

"You do?"

Michael faced her. "Shouldn't I?"

"Yes, of course. I'm totally trustworthy." She grinned at him. "But we haven't really known each other that long . . . I wouldn't blame you if you were skeptical."

Michael didn't say anything, and once again they fell into silence. Diamond sat back.

She wasn't sure if she could get used to Michael. Sometimes, he seemed willing to talk to her. Other times, he put up a wall and left her on the other side of it. Was this how he was on a day-to-day basis? Or only with her?

Sure, they didn't really know each other, but

they'd spent nearly a day together. Couldn't he find something to say to her?

After a long while driving, Michael faced her and asked, "Where was your car?"

Diamond looked beyond him to the westbound stretch of the highway. "Gosh, I'm not really sure. I only know that I was getting fairly close to Naples at the time we pulled off the road."

"Hmm."

" 'Hmm' what?"

"I don't see your car."

"Then it's gotta be farther up the road," Diamond said. Though she could have sworn she had already passed the exit for the Indian reservation yesterday, which would mean the car should be behind them.

Michael continued to drive, passing the reservation by several miles. Diamond saw her confusion mirrored on his face. "I know I wasn't this far from home when you hit me," he said.

"No, I don't think so."

Michael slowed, and though the median was reserved for emergency vehicle turns only, he made a U-turn and headed in the opposite direction. Diamond kept her eyes glued to the right shoulder.

When they once again reached the exit for Naples that would lead to Michael's house, she knew they hadn't made a mistake.

"My car," she said on a whimper. "It's gone."

CHAPTER SIX

Michael exited the interstate and pulled his car into the first service station he saw. Once there, he killed the engine and turned in his seat to face Diamond.

But she didn't meet his eyes. Instead, she dragged a hand over her face in frustration, then got out of the car. Michael watched as she did a slow three-hundred-sixty-degree turn, as if she expected to see her vehicle parked somewhere near here.

Groaning, she threw her hands in the air, letting them drop to her thighs. "I can't believe my car's missing! This is the last thing I need."

"I doubt it's *missing*," Michael assured her, stepping out of the car so he could talk to her. "But it was probably towed." Cops routinely had abandoned cars towed off the road. Usually, they would wait at least a day to do so, or even two. Which is what Michael had expected.

"I had everything in there. My makeup. My clothes . . ." She moaned.

"And you'll get it back. It's just going to take a bit longer than you originally thought."

She looked across the car's hood at him, a hint of desperation in her eyes. "What if it's been stolen?"

Michael shook his head. "I highly doubt that. Your car was left on the shoulder. Most people would assume it was inoperable—a waste of time trying to steal."

"It's a late-model Acura."

"Even late-model cars have their problems."

Diamond turned, pacing a few steps. She spoke as she talked. "It could have been taken for parts. The car has expensive, flashy rims. Goodness, what was I thinking?"

"You weren't thinking that you'd get into an accident and have to leave it on the side of the road. But I'm telling you, don't worry. I'm certain it was towed somewhere."

Diamond sighed. "I hope you're right, Michael. But I still need my stuff. Brother."

"The only thing we can do now is head back to my place and make some calls to find your car. There aren't that many places in the city where the car could have been towed. I'll call around. Don't worry. We'll find it."

"Right. I'm sure you know what you're talking about. I guess I just wanted to hit the road as soon as possible."

"Sorry. You're stuck with me a while longer."

Diamond stopped pacing and looked at Michael. A hint of a smile lifted his lips, but it didn't give anything away. "I'm not in a hurry to get away from you," she clarified.

"Good to hear."

Diamond frowned slightly. Last night, she would

have sworn that Michael couldn't wait to be rid of her. Today, he was sending her a different signal.

"I'm going to need toiletries," she said. "Clean underwear . . ." She couldn't very well borrow anything of his. And she would definitely need to shower.

"And I need some groceries. We'll make a stop at the Publix near my house and pick up some stuff."

Diamond nodded absently.

"This is a delay," Michael said, "but not a long one. It's not the end of the world, Diamond."

Diamond shrugged as she faced him. "Guess there's nothing else I can do."

"Not standing here, there isn't. The faster we get back on the road, the faster we can get this all straightened out."

"Right." Diamond made her way back to the car and got inside. So did Michael. Less than a minute later, he was driving out of the service station and heading back onto the road.

"You know your license plate number, right?" he asked.

"Of course."

"Hey, I had to ask. I've met a lot of people who didn't know."

"I guess the world takes all types."

"It sure does."

Diamond's mind wandered to Clay at her comment. He was definitely a wacko, but unfortunately, the world had its share of those, too.

She wondered where he was now. Had it been him she had seen yesterday on the highway? Or was he in Miami, staking out Coral Gables? As far as she knew, he didn't know where she lived, but people were extremely resourceful these days.

Especially criminals.

The car came to a stop, and Diamond looked up. She was surprised to see that they were in the parking lot of the grocery store. She had totally zoned out on the drive.

As they both exited the car, Diamond said, "I'll meet you in the grocery store."

"Oh?"

"Yeah. I'm gonna head into that little discount shop for some personal items." Like new underwear and another outfit. "Just in case it takes longer to find my car than I hope."

"Sure."

Michael and Diamond headed their separate ways. Inside the discount clothing store, Diamond perused the racks for generic clothing items she could purchase quickly. She found a couple of casual T-shirts and skirts and some underwear. But on her way to the cashier, she spotted a summery orange dress that tied around the neck like a halter top. It also boasted a killer slit up the front.

It was just her style . . .

"Need some help?" a saleswoman asked.

"Actually, yes. I'd like to try these on." She glanced around. On a nearby mannequin, there was a bright pink cutoff T-shirt with matching pink shorts. "And if you have that outfit in a medium, I'd love to try that, as well."

"No problem," the dark-haired woman told her. "The change rooms are at the back of the store. I'll bring the other outfit to you there."

Grinning widely, Diamond hurried to the change rooms. Shopping was one of her favorite things to do. Inside a stall, she hung everything up and began to disrobe.

She tried the casual skirts first, making sure they

fit. They did, which she had expected. There was no need to try the T-shirts.

"Here you go," she heard the saleswoman say; then the pink top and matching shorts appeared over the change room door.

The shorts were ... short. But Diamond liked sexy, and she had the physique to pull it off. She worked out regularly, making sure to keep her body in tip-top shape.

She reached for the dress. It was conservative and provocative at the same time, and she knew it would look great on her.

She slipped the dress over her head. Like many stores, there were no mirrors in the actual change room, which meant she had to step outside her stall in order to see how she looked in the outfit.

"That looks amazing on you," the saleswoman said as Diamond exited the stall. Diamond knew it was the standard sales pitch, but this time, she agreed. As she approached the nearby mirror, she couldn't help smiling. The dress fit her as if it were made for her, following her curves and flowing out around her knees.

"I have these great strappy orange sandals that will look amazing with this dress."

"High or low-heeled?" the woman asked.

"High. And sexy as all hell."

"I'm sure they make you look like a knockout."

"Yes, I'm sure they do."

At the sound of Michael's voice, Diamond's heart slammed against her chest. She whirled around and saw him standing several feet away from her.

"Michael." She felt flustered. "I didn't know you were here."

"Just got here. I came in to find you." He paused.

"And I'm glad I did." His eyes slowly roamed her body. "That dress is something else, Diamond."

Diamond's face grew warm. "Thanks."

"Are you getting it?"

"Yes," she told him. "That and a few other things."

"Other outfits to model?"

Did he *want* her to model for him? The very thought made her entire body grow warm. She could easily imagine modeling for him. But not here. Somewhere private.

"No, I . . . I'm finished trying on outfits. Give me a minute. I'll get changed."

"Sure."

Diamond hustled back into her change room, her heart beating a mile a minute. Lord help her, there was something about Michael that brought out a carnal reaction in her. But she truly didn't understand the man. She never would have expected him to say something so . . . so suggestive to her. He pretty much seemed all business where she was concerned.

Or maybe, that was what he was trying to make her think.

Maybe Diamond wasn't crazy to believe that she felt a spark between them.

As she changed, she wondered if Michael stood outside, imagining her with her clothes off the way she had tried to picture what he looked like naked while in the shower.

Get a grip, Diamond! You have to stop thinking these crazy thoughts.

Instead of changing into the clothes she had worn into the store, she slipped into the hot-pink shorts and T-shirt. She couldn't lie to herself. She wanted to see Michael's reaction to her in this outfit.

He glanced her way the moment she stepped out of the change room, and was rewarded with the undeniable look of attraction that sparked in his eyes. They first widened, as though with shock, then narrowed in a way that told her he was definitely noticing her as a woman.

"I was figuring I'd also buy this," Diamond told him. "What do you think?"

Michael cleared his throat loudly. "Not much to that one."

"But you like it?"

Uncomfortable, Michael turned away. Diamond was undoubtedly an attractive woman, the kind a man normally had no trouble looking at, but seeing her in those short shorts with her midriff exposed—and barefoot, to boot—disturbed him. Because something happened when his eyes roamed the long expanse of her well-toned legs. Something he hadn't been prepared for.

His groin had tightened.

Since well before Debra had left, Michael hadn't looked at a woman in the way he had just looked at Diamond. It was the kind of look that led to something else, something he considered dangerous. If they were somewhere else—alone—God only knew what could happen if she pranced around half naked in front of him, trying to turn him on.

Because he was pretty sure that that was what she was trying to do—turn him on.

Or was that simply wishful thinking on his part?

"I'll change now," Diamond said, interrupting his thoughts. Geez, even her voice seemed low and seductive. "I won't be but a minute."

"Sure." Michael swallowed. "I'll, uh . . . head outside and wait for you."

He didn't face her as he said the words, instead already placing one foot in front of the other to take him away from her. He desperately needed some fresh air.

Outside, Michael inhaled deeply and placed his hands on his hips. Good Lord, what was going on with him? He had seen plenty of attractive women since Debra had left him and Ashley had died. But he'd felt nothing for any of those women. Which was the way he wanted it. He wanted to forever be able to turn off his emotions. That way, he would never have to deal with pain again.

So why on earth had Diamond stirred something deep inside him?

Maybe it simply had been too long since he had been with a woman, and his body was reacting in a primal way to someone he found attractive. Which, he conceded, was normal. Even if he didn't like it.

What mattered most was that he understood the vulnerability. Understood and acknowledged it, so that he didn't fall prey to it.

At the sound of the store's door, Michael turned in that direction. Diamond stepped outside, saying, "Sorry. I didn't mean to take so much time."

"No problem."

"I guess you've already finished shopping?"

"Uh-huh."

"Oh. Well, I really hate to ask, but since we're already here . . . would you mind if I head into Publix and pick up some foundation and lipstick? And maybe some eyeliner, too."

"Diamond, don't you have all that in your car?"

"Yes, but I don't have it with me, and I haven't

tracked down my car yet. I want to look present-able.''

"Presentable?''

"Yes,'' she responded weakly. She suddenly real-ized that she sounded vain. The truth was, she normally didn't care how she looked at home, but in public, she preferred to wear at least some basic makeup. And she felt the urge much more in front of Michael.

"Whatever you say.'' Michael shrugged. "But as far as I'm concerned, you don't need all that stuff. You look beautiful without it.''

Beautiful . . . Diamond's heart slammed against her rib cage at Michael's compliment. Had the words just slipped off his tongue, or did he actually mean them?

"Well . . .'' There was a time when Diamond couldn't accept a compliment without saying some-thing like "Really?'' or "But I'm so tired today, I'm sure I have horrible bags under my eyes.'' However, she had been told on more than one occasion that she needed to simply accept a compliment.

So she said, "Thank you.''

"I mean it,'' Michael added, as though he had read her mind. "Women spend a lot of money on all this *stuff* to beautify themselves, and most of the time, it's a waste.''

"I guess I've accepted what society says—that a woman should always look her best.''

"Well, you've got no one to impress out here.''

While only moments before, Diamond's heart had beat with excitement, she now felt a stab of disappointment. What was Michael saying—that he didn't care if she bought makeup because she could never impress him?

She sucked in a sharp breath. She had to stop psychoanalyzing his every word and action.

"All right," she conceded. "I should find my car soon enough, anyway. I suppose there's no reason to buy more makeup at this point."

"Exactly."

Plus, she wanted to shower and change into one of her new outfits.

"You ready to head back to my place?" Michael asked.

Diamond smiled. "Sure."

CHAPTER SEVEN

The moment Michael and Diamond returned to his place, Michael headed straight for the phone. Keeping busy was something he needed to do right now, so he was glad that he had to call the city's auto shops and find out where Diamond's car had been taken.

Michael had the living room phone in his hand when he saw Diamond turn in the hallway and walk in the direction of the front door. "Hey," he called. "Where are you going?"

She poked her head into the living room moments later. "I'm just gonna walk around outside. What, are you afraid I'm gonna find all the hidden graves in your backyard?"

"Very funny. I was just curious. Take your time and enjoy yourself. You'll soon realize why I love this place so much."

"Okay."

"By the time you get back, I hope to have located your car."

Diamond nodded; then she was off.

Michael replaced the receiver and reached for the telephone directory beneath the phone's table. He was going to need it in order to find the list of auto repair shops.

He opened the book to the yellow pages, found the listing of auto repair shops, and dialed the first one.

Diamond was more impressed than she thought she would be as she strolled the grounds of Michael's property. There was a large backyard patio area that would be perfect for entertaining. It included an in-ground pool and hot tub. But that wasn't what made the greatest impact on her.

It was the serenity of the place, plain and simple.

Considering how hectic her life had been running from Clay, she was enjoying the peace and quiet of Michael's home. She walked through the grove of trees, listening to the sound of chirping birds and the gentle rustling of the leaves in the slight breeze. An aura of tranquillity swept over her. Why did she never take the time to walk on the beach and simply enjoy nature? Her cousin Tara lived in a community with a walking path that surrounded a lake, and if she wanted, Diamond could enjoy the quiet beauty nature had to offer there. But she was always on the go, always hustling to work or to some event.

The thicket of trees went back several feet, so far that Diamond wasn't sure where his property ended. She wondered if he planned to knock down some of these trees and put something else in their place. But as soon as that thought formed in her mind, she dismissed it.

It was obvious that Michael was a very private person, and this place suited him very well.

Fallen branches crunched beneath Diamond's feet as she turned and headed back toward the house. The wind picked up, and she hugged her torso against the sudden chill. It was January, and while the sun shone brightly, there was a chill in the air.

Diamond's thoughts suddenly went to Clay. She ran her hands over her arms trying to warm herself, but the chill now seemed to be coming from within.

Nervously, she glanced around. She felt him here. *Was* he here, lurking among the trees? Was he somewhere nearby, watching her?

Diamond swallowed, her throat thick. But how could that be? There was no way that Clay knew she was here.

Or was there?

Diamond . . .

Her name seemed to float on the wind, making her more fearful than before. Good Lord, what if Clay really was out here? What if he had truly tracked her down?

Diamond's heart rate accelerated as fear spread through her body, and she started running back toward the house. Something snagged at her dress, and she let out a scream and began to struggle, until she realized that it was a branch that had latched on to her.

As she knocked the branch away from her, she heard her name again. It was louder this time, and as she spun around, she saw Michael rushing toward her.

"Michael." Relieved, Diamond ran to him and threw herself into his arms. Michael immediately secured his arms around her, and Diamond instantly felt safe.

"What happened, Diamond?" he asked, concern lacing his voice. "Are you okay?"

"I-I don't know . . . I just . . . I heard something and . . . I guess I got scared."

Michael ran a hand over her hair. "It's all right now, Diamond. I told you I wouldn't let anyone hurt you, and I won't."

Maybe she was crazy, but she believed him. She believed that this man whom she had known for such a short time would do whatever it took to keep her safe.

Resting her face against his strong chest, she sighed. It was startling how safe she felt in Michael's arms. Startling how much she wanted to stay right where she was and let him make her feel secure forever. With Paul, Diamond had practically resented his masculine desire to protect her. But then, maybe she had sensed something wasn't right with Paul, sensed that he'd do the unthinkable where she was concerned in order to get his way.

It was different with Michael. With him, Diamond appreciated his quiet strength.

"I feel so silly," Diamond admitted. "I'm already on edge, and like a fool, I got spooked."

"It happens," Michael said. "There's no need to beat yourself up."

"True enough."

Michael pulled back and looked down at her. "You feel better now?"

"Yes."

"Ready to get your car?"

Diamond's eyes lit up. "You found it?"

"Yep. If you want, we can head out to get it right now."

Get my car, then what? Diamond wondered. Leave, never to return?

She asked, "You mean leave *right* right now?"

"You said you wanted to hit the road, didn't you?"

Diamond felt a sinking sensation in her stomach. Just moments ago, she was enjoying the feel of being in Michael's arms. She was enjoying the way he had told her he would make sure to keep her safe. Now, he sounded like he wanted to get rid of her.

But even if that was the case, why should that bother her? After all, she had been saying that she wanted to hit the road as soon as possible.

"Well, I . . ." She paused. "I was thinking that I'd take a shower first and change." That wasn't a lie. "Especially if I'm going to head off right away. So, maybe I should do that first. Then we can go get my car."

"You want to take a shower?"

"If you don't mind."

"I don't mind. That'll give me a chance to make some breakfast. You like omelets?"

"Mmm-hmm."

"I picked up ham, onions, cheese, green peppers, and mushrooms. How does that sound?"

"Sounds scrumptious already."

Michael and Diamond slowly walked back to the house. They entered through the back door, which led them into the back end of the hallway.

"You know where the bathroom is," Michael said. "Towels are in the linen closet."

"Great. Let me get my bag of purchases." She scurried ahead several feet to the door and retrieved her bag.

"By the time you get out of the shower, the omelets will be ready."

"I can't wait," Diamond told him, then turned and headed for the bathroom.

Diamond couldn't deny it—the omelet Michael had prepared was probably the best omelet she had ever eaten. Certainly, it was better than any she had ever made. Not that she could claim to be a culinary genius by any means.

She glanced at Michael's profile as he drove to the auto shop. The man was gorgeous *and* he could cook. Why was he single?

Diamond wanted to ask him exactly that, but bit her tongue. The radio was playing soft jazz, and she didn't want to ruin the mellow mood by prying into his personal life. And it was nice to sit back and listen to music, rather than feel she had to fill every waking moment between them with chatter about one subject or another.

But there was another reason Diamond kept quiet. She had the strange feeling that Michael was doing everything in his power not to look her way. Ever since she had come out of the shower wearing the pink shorts and T-shirt, Michael had been suspiciously silent.

She knew he was a brooding type, a deep thinker, and she didn't doubt that he had a lot on his mind. But she also hadn't missed his initial reaction to her in her new outfit, though she had pretended not to notice. As she had padded barefoot into the living room, she had seen Michael's eyes widen and his bottom jaw drop. The reaction had caused a frisson of heat to zap her body in its most intimate place, knowing that he found her attractive.

Diamond had stood there, staring at him, waiting to see if he would say something. Instead, Michael had looked back at the television before asking if she was ready to leave. Even as he'd gotten to his feet and walked toward her, he had avoided looking at her. And when he did look her way, he made sure to keep his eyes on her face.

Put it out of your mind, Diamond told herself. Michael would only be in her life for a short time, and as appealing as he was, she did not want to do anything to encourage their physical attraction. Sure, she knew the outfit she'd bought didn't help, but she hadn't been able to resist. She was still a woman, and it was a wonderful feeling to know that you could turn a man to putty simply by how you appeared physically.

The right man, of course.

Sighing softly, Diamond turned her attention to the scenery as they drove. Their bellies full from the late breakfast Michael had prepared, they were now on their way to pick up her car.

Several minutes later, Michael slowed the car and turned into a driveway. Diamond looked up to see that they had pulled into the parking lot of a business called Roy's Repairs.

Michael parked the car and they both got out. Michael took the lead, heading into the establishment and walking right up to the front counter. There was only one person there, to whom Michael said, "Are you Roy?"

The man looked at Diamond first, then at Michael. "Yes."

"I spoke with you on the phone," Michael explained. "I'm the one who called about the car that was towed here."

Something unreadable flashed in the man's eyes. "Yes, that's right," he replied.

"Great." Michael glanced at Diamond, and she smiled. "Now, I know the car had some damage, so do you have a quote for how much it will cost to repair?"

"Uh . . . sure." His eyes flitted between Michael and Diamond. "I know I printed it out somewhere. Give me a moment to go look for it."

Michael had been off the job for a while, but he knew his cop instincts were still dead-on. This guy was on edge for some reason, and Michael wanted to know why.

"Can't you access it from your computer with the license plate number?"

"Well, uh, since I already printed it, I may as well find that sheet of paper. One sec."

Roy started to turn, but Michael asked, "Everything okay?"

"Yeah. Sure." Roy dragged a hand over the back of his neck as he faced them again. "Why wouldn't it be okay?"

"I don't know. You seem . . . tense. Preoccupied."

"It's one of those days, ya know? I've got a lot on my mind."

Michael nodded his understanding, but his gut still told him something more was going on. He watched Roy hurry into the back office.

"Michael, what is it?"

Michael bit down on his bottom lip before speaking. "I'm not sure. But I'm not getting a good vibe from this guy. He seemed pretty nervous, don't you think?"

"I don't know." Diamond shrugged. "Maybe. But even if he is, what could that matter?"

"That's what I'm trying to figure out."

"You think he's some kind of con artist?"

"This shop has a good reputation, from what I know. It's the way he's looking at us. I'd bet my life something is wrong."

"But what could be wrong?" Diamond asked. "I mean, the guy doesn't know us. It's probably something else going on. Who knows? Maybe he even had a fight with his girlfriend."

"That's not the vibe I'm getting."

"If you don't feel comfortable with him, when he comes back, we'll just tell him that we want to take the car to another shop. No big deal."

Michael didn't respond. Instead, his eyes narrowed on something behind her, and she saw concern written on his face in big, bold letters.

Whirling around, she followed his line of sight.

Through the floor-to-ceiling windows, she saw two police cruisers skidding to a stop outside the front door. Then four cops were rushing out of the cars and into the shop.

A sense of panic filling her, Diamond glanced at Michael. He stood, seemingly transfixed, no doubt wondering what was going on.

"Is this them?" the female cop asked.

"Yep."

Michael and Diamond spun around to see the mechanic standing behind the service counter once again. What the hell was going on?

"Diamond Montgomery?"

"Yes." Diamond's voice was soft, vulnerable, and Michael had the strongest urge to take her in his arms and protect her.

"Will you come with us, Miss Montgomery?"

Michael stepped forward. "Wait a second. What's going on?"

One of the male cops immediately stepped into Michael's path, holding out an arm to keep him at bay. "This will all go smoothly if everyone cooperates."

"We need to ask Ms. Montgomery some questions," another cop replied.

"What kind of questions?" Michael wanted to know.

"Is this about Clay?" Diamond asked.

"It's about your car," the female cop answered. "Now, if you'll step outside with us."

Diamond threw a glance over her shoulder at Michael. He saw panic in her eyes. All he could do was shrug.

Diamond stepped forward. The female cop extended a hand to keep Diamond from getting too close. With her other hand, she reached behind her back and produced a pair of handcuffs.

Stopping, Diamond went stiff.

Michael hustled toward her, but two of the three male cops quickly blocked his path.

Frustrated, Michael asked them, "What the hell is going on here?"

"This is just a precaution."

"What kind of precaution?" Michael demanded.

"Sir, you're not helping the situation," one of the male officers told him.

"Are you arresting me?" Diamond sounded horrified.

"We just want to make sure there aren't any problems," the female officer replied. "If you can place your hands behind your back and turn around."

Michael watched as Diamond complied. These cops weren't going to give him any answers, so he spun around to face Roy. "What, you called the cops?" The mechanic glanced away. "Why?"

"I don't want any trouble," he finally replied, still not meeting Michael's eyes.

"Could have fooled me." Michael turned to see the female officer and another cop walking Diamond outside as if she were some common criminal. He had done the same thing before—temporarily detained someone while conducting an on-the-scene investigation. But what on earth could be going on here?

One of the two male officers still inside approached the mechanic. "Where's the car?"

"Right back here."

"The drugs are inside?"

"Found 'em right on the floor behind the passenger seat, and that's where I left them. I didn't want to touch 'em and mess up any evidence, ya know."

"Drugs?"

The shorter cop faced Michael then. "Yes, drugs. Now, you need to stay back while we conduct our investigation. Or you'll be in as much trouble as your friend apparently is."

CHAPTER EIGHT

Ignoring the warning to stay back, Michael strode purposefully toward the officers. They were now at the door that led to the work area of the shop. "Look, you can talk to me. I'm a cop."

The taller of the two cops turned to him. "You are?"

"Yeah. Have been for over five years. I'm on a leave of absence right now, but I work in Fort Lauderdale." He still carried his warrant card with him—the photo ID that identified him as a police officer in the City of Fort Lauderdale—so he reached into his back pocket and produced it. "I can give you the name of my captain to call, if you want further verification."

Both cops inspected the ID. Then the shorter one asked, "This woman's a friend of yours?"

"Yes. And I can assure you, she would not have drugs in her car. Her car broke down yesterday, so she left it on the shoulder of the highway. If there are drugs in there now, that means someone must have gotten into it." Michael might not have known Diamond well, but he absolutely did not believe she was into anything illegal. "This is a big misunderstanding."

The taller officer nodded. "I hear what you're saying."

"But you don't believe me."

"I didn't say that. We were called here to investigate this matter, and that's what we need to do. We'll figure this out. If you don't mind sitting tight for a few minutes, that will give us time to do our job."

Michael wanted to say something else, more words to assure them of Diamond's innocence, but he knew that wouldn't do any good. The best thing he could do was cooperate with them, because neither he nor Diamond had anything to hide. So he said, "Of course."

"Thank you."

With chagrin, Michael stood back and watched the officers from the sidelines.

"Drugs?" Diamond asked, completely perplexed. "I have never touched any type of drug in my life!"

"We got a call from the owner of the shop. He said he found drugs in the car, and that the owner was here."

So that's why the man had seemed to be stalling them. Michael had been right—Roy *had* been on edge.

"If there are drugs in my car, they aren't mine. Honestly."

"Drug running along I-75 is a fairly big problem," the female officer said, as if she didn't believe Diamond. "One we're trying to crack down on."

From the backseat, Diamond looked first at the female cop, then at the male one. This whole situation seemed so bizarre, she would swear she was having a nightmare. But she wasn't. This was really happening. "That car has been out of my care and control for nearly twenty-four hours," Diamond pointed out. "Surely there's no way you can say the drugs are mine."

"Care and control," the male officer repeated. "Let me guess, you're a *Law and Order* fan?"

"Or a woman who's already been charged with a drug offense."

"My ex is a cop," Diamond said directly to the female officer, feeling a tad miffed that she was forced to defend herself for something she hadn't done. "So I know a thing or two."

"Then you know that in a situation like this, we've got to investigate in order to get to the bottom of what's going on."

"I will gladly answer any of your questions," Diamond told the woman. "Just—just don't treat me like a criminal."

"Why don't you tell us what happened?" the male asked.

Diamond inhaled deeply, then spoke. "I was driving—"

"Your ID says you live in Miami," he interjected. "What were you doing heading this way?"

"I . . . I was just driving, not sure where I was going." When both cops looked at her with curiosity, Diamond went on. "This is the deal. There's a guy who's after me. Clay Horton. Over two years ago, he tried to abduct me and was subsequently arrested. There was a trial, he was found insane and locked up. He's just escaped from custody. I knew he was heading to Miami to find me, so I packed up my car and left. Yesterday, as I was driving, I thought I saw him following me. I ended up in a fender bender and left my car at the side of the road. Michael picked me up," she added, not letting the cops know that she and Michael hadn't known each other before.

"Why didn't you arrange to have your car towed?"

"Because it was still drivable. But *I* was in no state to drive. Michael figured I should take some time to decide where I was going and to calm down. So I went to his place. We went back to get the car a few hours ago and discovered it was gone." She paused. "You don't believe me, do you?"

"We're simply collecting facts right now," the female replied.

Collecting facts, my butt, Diamond wanted to say. If that was the case, then why did they have her handcuffed, like they were ready to cart her off to jail?

Instead, she said, "Think about it. If I had drugs in my car, why would I leave them? That would be pretty stupid of me for many reasons—including if the car got towed. I don't even know what kind of drugs they are."

"Fraser," the female officer said, "you want to go in there and see what's happening?"

"Sure."

When the male cop was out of the car, Diamond asked, "Are you arresting me?"

"We'll figure it all out in a little while."

Resigned to her fate, Diamond sat back. And for the first time, she contemplated the reality of the situation.

Drugs in her car? It was completely absurd. Either

the mechanic had gotten the wrong car, or something bizarre was truly going on.

All she could do now was wait. And have faith that this would all work out the way that it should.

When the two male officers reentered the customer waiting area, Michael got to his feet and started toward them. "Well?"

"Heroin," one replied, holding up a clear plastic bag.

"Heroin?" Good Lord, that was serious. He was hoping that at worst, the car had a bit of marijuana. "And you're sure it was in Diamond's car?"

"The black Acura is her car, isn't it?"

"Yeah, but—"

"But," the taller cop interrupted, "we realize that the car wasn't in her possession for the better part of a day. Which means someone else could have put the drugs in her car, no matter how strange that sounds."

"Someone else *did* do that."

"A charge against her would never hold up in a court of law," the officer conceded. "Plus, the manager here told us something interesting. Apparently, someone called and told him to check the car for drugs. Given that and the apparent vandalism—"

"Wait a second." Michael held up a hand. "Vandalism?"

"He'll explain all the damage to you, but it's pretty extensive."

Michael ran a hand over his head. What on earth was going on? Who in his right mind vandalized a car parked on the side of the highway?

In his right mind . . . Good grief, could it be Clay?

But how could it be? Diamond had been afraid yesterday, feeling she had seen him. Michael had dismissed the sighting as a paranoid reaction.

Yet if someone had vandalized the car, had put drugs in it . . .

When the cops headed outside, Michael followed them. One of them made his way to the driver's side of the cruiser, where the female officer sat. After conversing with her for a long moment, the female got out of the car and opened the back door. She helped Diamond out.

"You're releasing her?" Michael asked.

As the woman unlocked Diamond's handcuffs, she replied, "Given the evidence, we can't hold her. A defense lawyer would easily chew up a charge against her and spit it out. Which you know, being a cop."

"Yes," Michael replied.

"Besides, this story has a lot of holes in it—like the anonymous call about the drugs."

"What?" Diamond asked.

"Someone apparently called and told the shop's manager that there were drugs in your car."

"Oh, my God." With her hands released, Diamond rubbed each wrist in turn. "How could that be? Who would—" But the question died on her lips as horror filled her eyes.

"Where can we reach you?" one of the male cops asked.

"My place," Michael chimed in. He stepped forward and gave the officer all his pertinent information.

"Great." He looked at Diamond. "We're releasing you for now, but ask that you remain in town, in case we have any more questions."

Diamond glanced at Michael, then at the officer who spoke. Her eyes said she was resigned to the situation. "All right."

Michael walked over to Diamond and placed a hand across her shoulders. "Don't worry, Diamond. We'll work this all out."

He felt Diamond relax, and a warmth he hadn't felt in a long time spread through him. The warmth of knowing that someone trusted him, that he was needed.

They watched the police officers get into their vehicles and drive away.

When they were gone, Diamond looked up at Michael, her bottom lip quivering. "He's here, Michael. I know Clay is responsible for this."

"Let's go back inside," Michael said. "I don't know if the officers told you, but your car was apparently vandalized."

"What?"

"That's what they said. We may as well find out how bad the damage is."

Groaning, Diamond allowed Michael to lead her back into the shop. Roy, who stood behind the counter, looked at them sheepishly. "I only did what I thought was right," he quickly said. "If those weren't your drugs, then I'm sorry."

Michael waved off the man's concerns. "I don't blame you for calling the police. It was the right thing to do."

"I'm glad you understand."

"My concern now is the car. The officers said it was vandalized?"

"It sure was."

Beside him, Diamond wrapped her fingers around his upper arm. "How badly?" she asked.

"There's a lot of damage," Roy replied. "The car isn't operable."

"You've got to be kidding," Diamond said.

" 'Fraid not."

"Great." Diamond moaned. Could her luck be any worse?

"What kind of damage?" Michael asked.

"Wires cut under the hood. And the battery's been smashed."

Diamond turned her face into Michael's arm. Michael glanced down at her, wondering if she was crying. He didn't think so.

He asked, "How long will that take to fix?"

The mechanic's expression wasn't hopeful. "We're talking quite a bit of work."

"Which you can't pay out of pocket," Michael pointed out. "You'll need to file a police report for insurance purposes."

"Who would do this?" Diamond asked, but her voice wasn't more than a whisper.

"You really think it was Clay?"

Diamond met Michael's eyes. "I don't believe that some random idiot decided to vandalize my car, no. I knew I saw Clay. And he's the one who did this." She whirled around, looking outside the windows. "Which means he could be anywhere near here . . . Oh, God. I-I have to get out of here."

Diamond started off, but Michael placed a firm hand on her shoulder, stopping her. "Hold up."

"What if this was all part of his plan?" Diamond asked frantically. "I can't stay here and be a sitting duck!"

Michael looked at her long and hard. Her beautiful eyes were filled with genuine fear. "You're really afraid of this guy, aren't you?"

"If he's vandalizing my car, what kind of message is he sending me? Please, let's just leave."

Michael turned to the mechanic. "We'll get back to you a little later, once she's filed a police report and contacted her insurance company."

"No problem," Ray said.

"In the meantime, if you can work out an estimate for the damage, that would be great." Michael picked up one of the man's business cards. "I'll be in touch."

"Sure thing."

"Michael, please," Diamond said. "We have to leave."

"I'm ready."

"Good." Diamond hustled to the door, and Michael followed her.

She had betrayed him.

And for that, she deserved to be punished.

When Diamond hadn't returned to her car yesterday, Clay had gotten a horrible feeling. His chest first tightened, making it hard for him to breathe; then a numbing sensation had spread down his arms and legs. As the hours had passed, a tension headache had built.

And when the tension built, he needed a way to release it. Now, he wanted to release it by giving Diamond what she deserved for betraying him—smacking her around until she begged for his forgiveness.

Clay didn't like feeling that way. He didn't like his violent thoughts. But he had tried to give Diamond the benefit of the doubt. He had wanted to believe that the man she had left with was someone who was simply helping her out. But how could he be, when Clay had driven the stretch of I-75 over and over again until the wee hours of the morning and she had not returned for her car?

That's when the tightness in his chest had started, and the throbbing in his head. His negative feelings could mean only one thing—that Diamond was off doing God only knew what with that man, betraying him the way she had betrayed him before. He had forgiven her the first time, but he could not forgive her now.

Vandalizing her car had brought him some relief for the tension pent up inside him. He would have smashed her car to pieces, if not for the traffic on the road. As it was, he knew he had done enough damage. Plus, sticking the bag of heroin under the seat was pure genius. If it got her locked up the way she had had him locked up, then Clay couldn't be happier.

With the damage to her car done, he had called the Florida Highway Patrol and anonymously reported that a car needed to be towed. He knew they would take it to Naples, the closest city.

The following morning, when he had called around to find out what garage the car had been towed to, he'd learned it wasn't in police custody. Meaning, they hadn't located the drugs. That's when he'd had the brilliant idea to anonymously report that Diamond had been carrying drugs in her car. The stupid witch deserved at least a few moments of stress, the way she had caused him two years of stress. It was a waste of good heroin, heroin he'd bought once he'd escaped, but it was worth it to make Diamond suffer.

All this thinking about her was giving him a headache. From his car parked across from Roy's

Repairs, Clay watched as she got into a car with that guy again.

He grabbed the empty soda can from the seat next to him and crushed it with one hard squeeze.

Diamond would pay for her whorish ways.

If it was the last thing he did, he would get back at her for ruining his life.

CHAPTER NINE

Michael was fairly quiet during the drive back to his place. Diamond knew he was deep in thought, as was she. But she was also a ball of tangled nerves, jittery and frightened over the new reality she was facing.

Clay was here.

Diamond glanced at Michael, and once again, she saw that the set of his jaw remained firm, the muscle in his jaw tense.

She made a concerted effort to steady her hands, then spoke. "I know this is much more than you bargained for. For Clay to vandalize my car and set me up the way he did . . . I think he's escalated further into insanity. God only knows what he's capable of. I wish to God I hadn't gotten you into this. If you can take me to a rental car company, or even somewhere where I can catch a bus—"

Michael faced her then. "Whoa, wait a second. You think I want you to leave?"

"Clay is out there, damn it!"

"Diamond, I know you're afraid, but while you're with me, Clay is not going to hurt you."

"But he's here, Michael. My God, how did he find me here?" She moaned softly. "The man is crazy. And as long as I'm with you, you're in danger."

"Did you hear what I said?"

"How on earth did he track me down? I need my car. I'm going to have to rent one."

"Diamond."

"I don't even know where I'm gonna go. But I can't go back to Miami. I have to head north."

"Diamond."

Her eyes flew to Michael's then, and she looked at him as though she was surprised to realize he'd been speaking.

"You can't leave yet—not with the issue of the drugs in the car."

"Oh, God. You don't think they'll be able to pin that on me?" Diamond's voice held a note of horror.

"No, not given the circumstances. But if you take off—even to run from Clay—you'll look suspicious."

"So I'm supposed to stay here and wait for him to come after me?"

"Clay won't hurt you. Not while you're with me."

Diamond exhaled long and hard. "I want to believe you, Michael."

"Then do."

"If you only knew Clay. He's probably following us right now!"

"I've dealt with psychos like him, Diamond. And I am a cop. I know how to be careful to avoid being followed."

Diamond turned in her seat and glanced out the back window. "You think so, too."

"Don't worry. If he followed us out of the shop, he's not following us anymore. I made sure to lose everyone around us."

There was a pause, then Diamond said, "That's why you made that series of turns."

"That's right."

Diamond nodded. "I guess I should have realized that you'd be thinking of that possibility."

Michael reached across the front seat and took her hand in his. "I know this is frightening, and yeah, it's not like any situation I've ever been in before, but we'll get through this."

Diamond glanced down at their joined hands, a strange warmth spreading through her. Maybe she was losing her mind, but being with Michael right now seemed . . . right. She wanted to ask why he was being there for her, when she wouldn't blame him for telling her she needed to leave.

He was a cop, had been in the military. Maybe it was simply his dedication to public service that made him feel like he couldn't turn his back on her.

Or was it something else?

Diamond leaned back in her seat and closed her eyes. She *was* losing her mind. How else could she explain her feelings of attraction for Michael at a time like this?

She tried to push thoughts of Michael out of her mind and concentrate on what she was going to do. Michael was clearly a gentleman and would never kick her out, but didn't she owe it to him to leave, making sure that if things got worse, he wouldn't be involved?

When Michael pulled to a stop in front of his

house, Diamond looked around. After several seconds, she was satisfied that Clay wasn't behind them.

"I told you, if he was following us, I lost him."

"For now," Diamond pointed out. "You're going to have to leave the property sometime, and if he was outside that auto shop, then he knows what you look like. Or what if he's clever enough to get your information from the police?" She whimpered. "Oh, Michael. I am so sorry to have gotten you into this."

"Don't worry about me."

"But how can you say that?"

"Clay will be a fool to even try to step foot on my property. Not that he'll ever find out where I live, but if he does, you need to know that I can handle him."

Not if he surprised them at night . . . Diamond held the thought inside. She wanted to believe Michael. And while she hadn't known him for very long, she knew that he would do what he could to keep her safe.

If he was physically able.

She drew in an unsteady breath. "I wish I knew how this happened."

"You think Clay is really the one behind this?"

"Who else could it be?"

Michael opened his car door. "Let's go inside."

"Yes, let's." If by any chance they had been followed, they would be much safer inside Michael's house as opposed to sitting in his car.

Diamond got out of the Honda. She glanced around warily, wondering if Clay was possibly somewhere in the shadows of the many trees in the vast yard. Just how desperate was he to get to her, and would he hurt Michael in the process?

Inside the house, Michael took Diamond's hand and led her to the living room. He brought her to the sofa, then said, "Sit."

"All concerns of the drug issue aside," Diamond began as Michael sat in the armchair across from her, "I'm more convinced than ever that I should hit the road."

"I think that's the last thing you should do."

"I will never forgive myself if something happens to you."

"Don't worry about me."

How could he sit there and say that? "I don't think you understand the seriousness of this situation. Clay is as psychotic as they come. But clever. God only knows how he managed to escape." Diamond shuddered. "And what if he's armed?"

"So am I."

A startled gasp escaped Diamond's lips.

"I'm a cop, remember?"

"Right. Of course." She was just so on edge, the thought of guns was making her jumpy.

"Let me guess—you don't like guns."

"What's to like about them?"

"Well, for one thing, if you know how to use them, they can be great for protection."

"And if people didn't have guns to begin with, no one would need them for protection."

"Did Clay use a gun when he attacked you?"

Diamond shook her head. "No, thank God." She paused. "Have you ever . . . used your gun?"

An unexpected chill ran down Michael's spine at the question. It was a harmless one, one many people asked cops, and he should have been prepared for it. But he saw the man in the alley, the flash of light, and remembered firing his weapon.

"You're suspended pending an IA investigation."

"Michael?"

"Yeah, I have. But I don't care to discuss the circumstances. However, I'll be more than happy to teach you how to fire my gun, if you wish."

Diamond's eyes registered shock. "Me, fire a gun? I don't think so."

"Women learn how to fire one every day to use for self-defense. I think it would be a smart move for you. Not just because of Clay, but you're a well-known radio personality. There may be other men like Clay in the future."

"Exactly what I don't want to hear."

"Understandably, but you have to face reality. This place is great because I have a lot of property, and a lot of trees. I've done some target practice out back from time to time."

"You don't kill birds, do you?"

Michael shook his head. "Of course not. I either shoot a target on a tree, or shoot bottles off a tree stump. There's no chance of anyone getting hurt."

Diamond looked at him like she didn't believe him.

Michael said, "Guns don't kill people—"

"People with guns kill people. Michael, honestly, I'm not up for a gun debate. The best I can do is agree they're a necessary evil."

Michael stood up. "I'm not going to force the issue, but if you want to learn how to handle one, I'll teach you. Personally, I think that's the first step in overcoming any reservations you have about guns."

He started to walk from the room, and Diamond asked, "Where are you going?"

"To the kitchen. I'm not going to leave you alone."

Diamond nodded. While her brain told her she

should hit the road and keep Michael out of her problem, she was secretly glad that he didn't want her to leave. She felt much better being here, being with him. She didn't know if she had the strength to deal with Clay alone this time around.

"Thanks, Michael."

"Make yourself comfortable. Try not to stress."

Michael knew that was easier said than done. Truth be told, he wondered how this creep had managed to find Diamond in Naples, wondered exactly what he was capable of. And despite his confident words to Diamond, he wondered if he'd have what it took to protect her when push came to shove.

He had told his captain that he needed to take a leave of absence from the force because he couldn't bear to have anyone second-guess him. But there was more to it than that. He couldn't bear to second-guess himself. What would happen if he went to a call where someone reportedly had a weapon, and instead of drawing his as he normally would, he paused, unsure of himself? Such moments of hesitation had gotten police officers killed. Michael knew he very well could face that situation.

Because the last thing he wanted to do was kill another unarmed man.

When are you going to forgive yourself?

"Easier said than done, Kelly," he mumbled.

Michael ambled farther into the kitchen, determined to shake the haunting memory. He opened the fridge and took out lettuce, a tomato, mustard, mayonnaise, and sliced ham. He spent the next several minutes preparing a ham sandwich for Diamond.

A short while later, Michael brought the sandwich and a glass of cola to her in the living room. She sat with her legs curled up on the sofa, her head resting on the armrest, her eyes closed. The sight of her in that provocative pink outfit gave him pause.

For a long moment, he simply stared at her. Lord help him, she really did have amazing legs. The drama over her car and Clay had made him forget about her incredible body. But seeing her lying there, quiet and beautiful, he couldn't help wondering what it would be like if she were a guest in his home under very different circumstances.

Damn, the thought surprised him. Here he was again, thinking about Diamond in a sexual way. Yet he hadn't thought of anyone in that way since Debra had left him.

Why Diamond, and why now?

Don't give it another thought, Robbins. He would not let his carnal feelings get the better of him. For one thing, he wasn't into casual sex. Yet if he were to let these feelings for Diamond build, that would be all he could offer her.

He could never offer her his heart.

Disappointed with the direction of his thoughts, Michael cleared his throat and moved his eyes to Diamond's face. "Diamond, here. Have something to eat."

Opening her eyes, she sat up. And smiled. A coy, sexy little smile if he ever saw one.

"You made me food?"

"A ham sandwich."

She reached for the tray, saying, "I'm not really hungry."

"Eat it anyway. You need it."

"You're right. Thank you." Diamond placed the

tray on her lap. She lifted one half of the sandwich and took a bite.

Michael watched her eat. Brother, but his body had a mind of its own. Watching Diamond flick out her tongue to capture mustard that landed on her lips was as erotic as watching a woman slowly disrobe.

This is what happens when you don't get any for a long time . . .

Even chewing had never seemed so sensual. Chewing, for goodness' sake. He had never gotten hot and bothered watching Debra eat, nor anyone else for that matter.

Diamond swallowed her mouthful of food, looked Michael squarely in the eye, and asked, "Why do you still want me here?"

Michael's stomach fluttered. Had she read his thoughts? Did she know that he had imagined her tongue flicking over his instead of that sandwich?

Diamond tilted her head to the side, narrowing her eyes. "Hmm?"

Lord help him, she *had* read his thoughts. Why else would she be flashing her flirty eyes at him now?

Great. How on earth was he going to talk himself out of this one?

CHAPTER TEN

Michael swallowed hard, stalling for time, then asked, "What do you mean?"

"I pretty much fell from the sky into your life," Diamond answered. "To put it nicely," she added with a smile. "I know it hasn't been easy. Forgetting the more serious issue, you seem like a very private person. That alone has to make this situation difficult for you. But instead of kicking me out, you want me to stay."

Maybe Michael was wrong. Maybe she hadn't read his thoughts. "What am I supposed to do? Abandon you?"

"I wouldn't blame you if you did."

He seemed to be in the clear. Thank God. Because he knew the attraction he felt for her wasn't one-sided, and the last thing he needed was for her to reciprocate what he was feeling by flirting with him.

"It's not going to happen."

"But why? I'm not trying to sound ungrateful— I totally appreciate all you've done. But I feel bad for dragging you into my problems. You figured you'd put me up for one night. Now, with today's turn of events, who knows how long I'll have to stay in Naples?"

"What's happened has happened."

Diamond paused a long moment as she sipped the cola. His words seemed to belie his outlook on his own situation. After all, if he was the "what's done is done" type, then why was he in Naples, on a leave of absence from his job? Diamond often got the distinct sense that he was running from something.

She looked at Michael and boldly asked, "What happened to bring you to Naples?"

Diamond watched his Adam's apple bob up and down. "I needed a break."

"What were you running from?"

"I didn't say I was running."

"You didn't have to. It's pretty obvious that something—"

Michael's eyes narrowed on her. "Listen, Diamond. I know you talk to people about their relationships, but don't try and psychoanalyze me, okay? While you're here, my personal life is off-limits."

"I only want to help."

"Is that so?"

"Yes."

Michael shot to his feet.

"What are you doing?"

"Leaving."

"Leaving? Where are you going?"

"For a walk. Last time I checked, that wasn't against the law."

Diamond stood. "Of course," she said softly. "Michael, please don't walk—"

Ignoring her, Michael all but ran to the front door. Air. He needed air. Outside, he drew in a shaky breath and gripped his side as he felt a sharp pain.

Damn the woman. He didn't want to talk about why he'd come to Naples, least of all with Diamond. He owed her no explanations. After all, *he* was doing her a favor.

And what did she think, that simply by talking about his problems they would all go away?

Michael may have believed that once, but life had taught him a very different lesson.

He charged down the front steps and got into his car. He wasted no time starting the engine. Jamming the car into reverse, he backed up so fast that he could see gravel and dust spitting up around him as he started to drive off.

Considering Clay didn't know where he lived, Michael was certain that Diamond would be safe at his home for the time he'd be gone. He needed to get away, to clear his head.

Michael loosened his grip on the steering wheel and tried to calm down. What was wrong with him, anyway? Was this how he would always be, flying off the handle every time someone asked him a question about his past?

His chest hurt, and it was hard to breathe. He felt angry and disillusioned at the same time. But the truth was, he couldn't say he was truly angry with Diamond. He was angry with himself.

Angry for wanting to feel differently, but having no clue how to go about it.

Kelly had always told him he was hiding out, which he had acknowledged. And he hadn't cared. . . . Was that starting to change? Did he want to reach out and touch the real world once again?

That very thought made him feel guilty. Ashley was dead. Hell, another man was dead on account of him, and here he was worrying about himself.

Michael continued to drive within the speed limit, though what he really wanted to do was push his Honda to its maximum velocity. He wanted to experience a tinge of danger and the rush that came with it.

He wanted to feel alive again.

Michael kept driving, not knowing where he was going until he turned into the driveway that led to his friend Jacob's house. Jacob, who had also suffered some devastating losses over recent years.

Jacob was the one he had talked to when he hadn't been able to turn to anyone else, because he knew that Jacob understood where he was coming from.

He needed to speak with Jacob now.

Michael rapped on the door for the third time. And wondered where Jacob was. His shift at the factory had ended over an hour ago, and Jacob Bush was the kind of man who got up, went to work, then came straight home. Michael knew, because many times over the past months, he had met Jacob after work, and the two had sat on the porch for hours, drinking a few beers and lamenting over everything that had gone wrong in their lives. Michael had met Jacob at an Alcoholics Anonymous meeting four months ago. Actually, he had met him outside the building. Jacob had been standing there, too afraid to go inside. Michael had been debating whether or not he should, himself. The two had gotten to talking and ultimately they had left, gone back to Jacob's house, and talked some more.

Michael didn't consider himself an alcoholic—though he knew that even the most hard-core, dependent drinkers didn't think themselves alcoholics, either. However, he did realize that he was starting to need liquor way too much in order to escape his pain. That's the reason he had voluntarily sought out an AA meeting, but he had also hoped to find people to talk to who would listen. People who didn't know him from Adam. He had found that in Jacob.

Unfortunately, Jacob had been drinking for years. The man wanted to change his ways, but couldn't seem to find the strength to do so. In the beginning, Michael hadn't minded sitting on the porch with him, sharing a brew, but it hadn't taken long for him to realize that it wasn't what he wanted for his life. So he had started to stay away more and more once he'd decided not to touch a drop of alcohol again, two months ago.

He felt bad for his once-in-a-blue-moon visits to Jacob, but he had also needed time to collect his own thoughts and put his life in perspective.

When Jacob still didn't answer the door, Michael's cop instincts grabbed hold of him. Had something happened? He checked the door. It was locked. He moved to the windows along the porch. No sign of forced entry.

He was about to head to the back of the house when he finally heard the shuffling of feet inside. A moment later, Jacob opened the door.

"Jacob," Michael said, partly relieved, partly concerned. "I've been knocking for minutes."

"I was sleeping. Sorry."

Either that or drunk. But Jacob was such a seasoned drinker that at this hour, he would still be wide awake. "Is this a bad time?"

Jacob shook his head, and Michael could see the imprint of the bedspread on the right side of his drawn face. So he had been sleeping, after all.

"All right." Michael stepped into the house and gave the older man a hug. "Everything okay?"

"Sure. I'm just getting old, is all."

Michael nodded. Was it his imagination, or did Jacob look slimmer? "Have you eaten?"

"Hmm."

"Is that a yes or a no?"

"I had some lunch at work."

"Which was what, five or six hours ago?"

"About that."

"But you've been drinking?"

"C'mon, Mike. You know I'm trying to quit. But I couldn't do it cold turkey like you did."

Michael sighed. He didn't want to push the man, but he was worried about him. "You have food in the fridge?"

"Uh-huh."

"Then why don't I make something for you?"

"That's not necessary."

"Yeah, it pretty much is," Michael mumbled. He wasn't ready to return home yet. To Jacob, he said, "Indulge me. I haven't been around to see you in a while, so this is something I want to do."

As it turned out, Michael had to buy some groceries for Jacob, whose refrigerator and cupboards were nearly depleted. He'd been right in his belief that Jacob wasn't eating properly.

"I've been buying lunch at work," Jacob had

protested when Michael told him that he had to take better care of himself.

In a way, it was as if Michael had become Jacob's father, making sure his friend was provided for. That saddened him, because Jacob was barely sixty. By most accounts, he was still young, but years of hard drinking had taken their toll on him.

Still, there was something different about Jacob. Unlike when Michael had first met him, he now looked drawn and weary. Sick, even. But when Michael had questioned him over the last couple of hours, he had vehemently denied that anything was wrong.

"You sure everything's okay?" Michael asked.

"Stop worrying about me," Jacob replied. He and Michael sat side by side in the rocking chairs on the porch. Jacob held an open beer can, while Michael nursed a soda. " 'Sides, I get the feeling something's going on with you."

Jacob was nothing if not intuitive. Michael had learned that soon after meeting him.

"Let me guess," Jacob said. "You plan on going back to work?"

Hearing the question, Michael cringed. He remembered the shooting, and for the zillionth time wondered if he would ever be ready to go back to work. "No, that's not it."

"Then what?"

Michael took a sip of his cola. "My world's been turned upside down in the past couple days."

"The one-year anniversary of Ashley's death had to be tough."

"Believe me, it was, but that's not all I'm referring to." He filled Jacob in on how he'd met Diamond, and what was currently happening.

"Wow. A real live psycho."

"Yeah."

"What are you gonna do?"

"The problem is, as much as I like my privacy, I can't very well tell her to hit the road. That wouldn't be right."

"Is that the only reason?"

Michael faced Jacob. He was surprised to see the man smiling at him.

"Oh, don't give me that look," Jacob said. "I may be a fool in many ways, but I was young once. I was in love with my dear Merline. God rest her soul."

"I'm not following you," Michael said.

"Like hell you're not, Mike. You're attracted to this woman, aren't you?"

Michael turned, looking out at the yard. It was full of weeds and unruly bushes. Maybe he'd come by one day and help put the place in order.

"If you're ignoring me—"

"I'm not ignoring you." Once again, Michael faced his friend. "All right. I'll admit, there's an attraction."

"And what about on her part?"

"I think so."

Jacob took a swig of his beer. "Then what's the problem?"

"The problem is . . . I'm not supposed to feel this way."

Jacob *tsked*. "Now why on earth would you say that? I know hanging with me hasn't helped give you the most positive view of the world, but if I was you, I wouldn't give up on it all. Not until you found your Merline. I had mine, so I've already had it all. That's been the hardest thing 'bout goin' on from day to day. Having to live without her."

He drank more beer. "But you . . . you still have something to look forward to."

"I'm not too sure about that."

"I'm old. Who knows how long I'll be around? That's why I don't care too much about curbing my bad ways. But you . . . you deserve better'n Debra."

Michael couldn't dispute that, but Jacob was taking this scenario way too far. "It's simply an attraction. I guess it disturbed me because I didn't expect to feel anything for anyone—at least not for a long, long time."

"She's at your place right now?"

"Yeah."

"Then what're you doin' here still?"

"I needed some time away from her. Some time to think."

"So this is serious."

Michael paused. "I don't know what it is." He only knew that whatever he felt for Diamond, it disturbed him.

Michael downed the last of his soda and stood. "I guess I'd better go."

"Come back and visit me soon."

"I will."

"Tell the young lady I said hi."

Michael couldn't help chuckling. It was weird, the relationship he had with Jacob. In so many ways, Jacob was wise. Yet when it came to his own life, he seemed incapable of behaving better.

As Michael got into his car, he waved to Jacob. He was already thinking about Diamond and seeing her again. There was something about her. A special and unique quality that drew him to her, even though he wanted to stay away.

Maybe he was simply horny. That could be a distinct possibility.

"Okay, Michael," he said to himself as he began to drive away from Jacob's house. "You're horny, and you want to make love. There's nothing wrong with that."

Which left him wondering what he was going to do. Should he try and seduce Diamond, if for no other reason than to get this lust out of his system? Or should he maintain his distance, knowing that casual sex wasn't his thing?

But damn if the idea didn't seem appealing now.

He would go with the flow, see where things led. That was all he could do.

But when Michael returned home, he found Diamond sleeping on the sofa. She looked so comfortable that he couldn't imagine disturbing her, not even to move her to the bed in his bedroom.

He went to his linen closet and withdrew a comforter. Just before he covered her barely clothed body, he allowed himself a good long look.

She truly did have amazing legs. Well toned; it was obvious she worked out. Her stomach was not only flat; she looked to have at least a four-pack.

His eyes roamed lower once again. With her legs bent, Diamond's shorts had pulled up to give him an enticing glimpse of the round curve of her butt.

An exquisite butt. Like the rest of her, it looked well toned. He wondered what she looked like naked.

Did her small breasts have large nipples, nipples that would immediately react to his touch, to his tongue? Lord help him, looking at her like this, he wanted to experience what it was like to make love to her. His body ached to be naked against hers, to know how they would be together.

Michael swallowed, then spread the comforter over Diamond's body. His thoughts had given him an aching erection.

Which was the last thing he needed, given the fact that Diamond was sleeping, and he would be heading to his bed—alone.

CHAPTER
ELEVEN

His heart pounding furiously in his chest,
Michael ran down the dark alley as if his life
depended on it. He jumped over broken bottles
and syringes and kicked empty beer cans aside.
There was so little light that he knew danger could
be lurking in the shadows, yet he couldn't give up.
He wouldn't let him get away!

So he ran through the alley until it met the side-
walk, feeling a modicum of relief that there were
at least some streetlights to help his search. He
paused only for a moment to see the direction the
perp had gone, and when he saw the long trench
coat billowing in the wind to the right, he pivoted
on his heel and continued the chase.

Suddenly the man stopped running and twisted
around to face him, and instantly the hairs on the
back of Michael's neck rose. *Danger!* a voice told
him, just as the guy reached for something inside
his coat.

Michael didn't have time to think, only act. He
did what he'd been trained to do, what he had

practiced so many times before. He withdrew his gun, aimed it at the target, and the moment he saw the flash of light, he fired.

The perp fell backward.

But when he ran to the man's side, looking for a gun or a knife, or any type of weapon, he saw only a small bottle of rum clutched in the man's hand.

"No!" There had to be a weapon somewhere. *There had to be.*

Michael wasn't sure what happened next, only that he was now facedown on the cold street. His breath ragged, his vision hazy, he looked around. Had someone hit him? How had he ended up on the concrete?

Not concrete, he realized, his brain clearing. *Hardwood floor.* The hardwood floor in his bedroom.

Good grief, he'd fallen out of his own bed!

He rose slowly, his heart racing from how vivid the dream had been. Here he thought he'd go to bed and dream of Diamond, dream of making hot, sweaty love to her, yet he had dreamed about the shooting, the one thing he wanted to forget.

He reached for the bedside lamp and turned it on, illuminating the room. Glancing at the wall clock, he moaned when he saw that it was shortly after six A.M.

Kelly had once suggested that he keep a journal of his feelings about the shooting and Ashley's death. He had blown off the suggestion without a second thought. Yet now . . . Now, he actually felt inspired to get his feelings onto paper.

It certainly couldn't hurt.

He got up and quietly went to the next bedroom,

the one he kept as an office. There he found a pen and a notepad, then sat at the desk's chair.

He started to write.

"What are you doing?"

Diamond spun around at the sound of Michael's voice. She flashed him a sheepish smile. "I'm sorry. I was hoping to surprise you with breakfast, but I've ruined it."

Michael sauntered into the kitchen, laughing.

"Don't laugh at me!" But truth be told, she couldn't blame him. And she was definitely happy to see him smiling. After last night, she wasn't sure he would be happy to see her this morning.

"What did you do to these eggs?" Michael asked. "They *are* eggs, right?"

"Of course they're eggs. They're just . . . a little burnt."

"Did you even put any oil in the pan?" Michael asked. "Forget it. I don't want to know."

Diamond's stomach sank. "Oil?"

"Yeah. You know, so the eggs wouldn't stick to the pan?"

"I thought they didn't stick."

"Maybe not on a Teflon pan, but this is a cast-iron skillet."

Diamond bit down on her bottom lip. She felt like a big moron. She had been hoping to make omelets, but had quickly amended that to scrambled eggs when she realized that she'd ruined the omelets. Then everything had started to stick to the pan, started to burn. What an idiot she was. Didn't every woman know how to cook eggs?

She angled her head to the side. "I never claimed to be a good cook."

"I never asked you to cook me anything."

"I normally have toast or cereal for breakfast, but the omelet you made was so yummy." Frowning, Diamond rested her butt against the counter.

"I can live on toast."

"Really?"

"Sure."

"Then toast it is." Diamond turned with gusto, then paused. "Uh, there is bread, right?"

"In the fridge."

"You have any peanut butter?"

"Yep."

"Grape jelly?"

"Actually, yes."

Diamond smiled widely. "A man after my heart."

A short while later, they sat at the small kitchen table eating their breakfast of toast and orange juice.

"I've got to tell you, Diamond. This is the best peanut butter and jelly toast I have had in ages."

"Hmm." Diamond eyed him with suspicion. "You don't have to lie, Michael."

"Who says I'm lying?"

She shook her head at him, a wry smile playing on her lips.

"I guess all I'm trying to say is, I appreciate your effort."

"No problem."

They ate in silence for a while; then Diamond said, "I'm sorry I upset you last night."

"Don't worry about it."

"You were gone for quite some time. And before

you say anything, I'm not trying to pry. I'm just making an observation. I feel bad, Michael. The last thing I want to do is force you out of your own home."

"You didn't. Last night, there was a friend I needed to see."

"Oh. Okay." *Male or female friend?* Diamond wondered. But she wasn't about to ask. So she decided to change the subject. "You know what I realized when you were gone?" Michael shook his head. "I was so upset yesterday that I forgot all about my luggage in the car." She looked down at the T-shirt she wore. She would need to pick up her clothes and personal items if she was going to be here much longer.

"Yeah, I realized that once we came back here. I have to give Roy a call today, anyway. To see how much damage has been done to your car. I figured we'd run by there and pick up your stuff. Speaking of which, we'll have to stop at the Florida Highway Patrol and file a report for insurance purposes. We may as well do that as soon as possible."

"Sure."

Now finished with her breakfast, Diamond got up from the table. She lifted her plate and glass and started walking to the sink.

"You didn't sleep in the bedroom last night," Michael said to her.

Diamond paused, but didn't turn around. She had been watching television and fallen asleep on the sofa. Sometime during the night, she had awoken and found the comforter over her. Right then, she had realized that Michael must be home and in his bedroom.

"I don't mind sleeping on the sofa," Diamond told him.

"But I do mind. As long as you're here, you sleep in my bed. Okay?"

It was merely a courteous offer, so why did it make Diamond's body ache with longing? Especially when he wasn't suggesting that she sleep in his bed with *him*.

Slowly, she faced Michael. There was no point in arguing. "All right."

They went to the police station first. Diamond filled out the appropriate police report, indicating that she had left her car on the side of the highway and that it had been vandalized. She also described the initial fender bender she had had with Michael, and mentioned Roy's Repairs as a point of contact for more detailed information on the damage. Of course, this report was for insurance purposes, so it was her insurance company that would follow up with questions, not the police.

A copy of the report in hand, Michael and Diamond then headed to Roy's Repairs. Another man was behind the counter when they entered. He gave them a bright smile.

"Hey," Michael said, nodding at the man. "We were here yesterday about an Acura that was towed in. We spoke with Roy."

"Roy's out back. I can get him for you if you like."

"Sure. That'd probably be best, since he knows about this situation."

"No problem."

Minutes later, Roy appeared at the front of the shop. When he saw them, he gave them a tentative grin. Clearly, he still felt bad about yesterday.

"Hi again." Michael spoke cheerfully, hoping to

allay any of the man's hesitation. "We're back with a police report, so you can start on the repairs to Diamond's car. Did you figure out the extent of the damage?"

"Well, the car's going to need a paint job, as the exterior was badly scratched. And with all the damage under the hood, you're looking at the four-thousand-dollar range."

"Four thousand dollars!" Diamond exclaimed.

"I'm sorry," Roy said. "I wish I had better news."

"What's your deductible?" Michael asked Diamond.

"Three hundred. Which isn't a big deal, but—" She turned back to Roy. "How long will it take for me to get my car?"

"I'm hoping a couple days. Maybe three, because the paint job will have to dry."

Three days. Three days spent in Naples, with Michael. Diamond's heart fluttered. Could they handle being around each other for three more days?

"You have your insurance information?" Roy asked.

"Uh, yeah." Diamond told him the name of her insurance company. "The policy number is in the car's glove compartment."

"All right. Let me get that; then you can sign the form authorizing me to do the work."

Diamond watched Roy walk away. And when she felt hands on her shoulders from behind, she jumped.

A moment later, she relaxed, knowing they were Michael's hands. She reached for his fingers, clasping them in her own.

"Three days isn't a long time, Diamond."

"I know. It's just that . . . I keep wondering, how

much more will Clay do to me? When is this all going to stop? And who knows if I'll be able to leave town when my car's repaired? The police may want me to stick around because of the drug issue.''

Michael turned Diamond to face him. She looked up into his eyes and was startled to see the tenderness there. She was even more shocked when Michael gently stroked her cheek.

''You still in a hurry to leave?''

Diamond was speechless. As she gazed into Michael's beautiful eyes, she had no clue what to say.

She wasn't sure if she thought or said the words, ''What's gotten into you?''

But when Michael replied softly, ''I don't know,'' Diamond knew she had spoken her thoughts out loud.

''I'm confused, Michael.''

''You're not the only one.''

''One minute you're—'' Diamond frowned as Michael stepped away from her. He looked over her shoulder. She turned, knowing Roy had reentered the room.

''All righty,'' Roy said, his tone upbeat. ''This is what I need you to sign.''

''Can I look at the car first?'' Diamond asked. ''Not that I don't trust you, but I suppose I ought to see the damage. . . .''

''Of course. Come on back with me.''

Diamond and Michael followed Roy to the back of the shop. When she saw her car, she gasped in horror.

''It looks worse than it is,'' Roy pointed out.

''It looks like a madman went at it.'' Which is exactly what had happened. Clay was as crazy as they came.

Diamond shivered. What would he have done if he'd actually gotten to her?

That thought making her pulse race with fear, Diamond walked closer to the car. She fingered one of the scratches and realized that it went very deep. She looked into the back of her car. Seeing some of her clothes lying haphazardly on the backseat and on the floor, she couldn't help wondering if Clay had gone through her personal items, as well as the police.

Groaning, she faced Roy. "What do you need me to sign?"

Roy passed her the paper and a pen. Diamond scribbled her signature on the form. Then she reached into her purse and extracted the car keys, which she handed to Roy.

"I can take out my stuff now?" she asked.

"Go ahead," Roy told her. "I'll leave you two to do that."

"Thanks," Michael told the man.

"I don't remember leaving my car unlocked. I know I could have, but I guess Clay just as easily could have broken in." Diamond moaned as she opened the back door behind the driver's seat. "It makes me sick to think he's been through this."

"He's not here now," Michael reminded her. "And he hasn't succeeded in his twisted plan to get to you, nor to get you arrested."

"Yet."

"Hey." Michael took her hand in his. "You're not going to do yourself any good thinking negatively. You have to believe that he won't succeed."

"That's what I'm praying for. It's just hard to keep the faith sometimes."

A stab of pain piercing his heart, Michael released Diamond. He placed his hands on his hips, trying to appear cool and calm. Diamond's comment hit too close to home, which was why he couldn't bring himself to respond to it. He didn't want to offer her empty promises like people had done with him.

While Michael still believed in God, he also believed that sometimes, despite faith, bad things happened.

He tried not to question God, but he was only human. He couldn't understand how God had taken Ashley at such a young age.

In the beginning, Michael had been very angry. Over the past months, he had tried to curb his anger because it was eating away at him. He had made progress, but it hadn't been easy. And the pain was always there.

"Michael?"

His eyes flew to Diamond's. She looked at him with concern.

"Michael, are you okay?"

All he could manage was a jerky nod.

"You're *not*." Diamond approached him. "What is it, Michael? What's wrong?"

He didn't say anything, merely looked away, but not before Diamond saw the haunted look in his eyes. She wanted to reach out to him, break down the barriers he had put around his emotions, but he had run when she'd tried to do that yesterday.

Instead, she placed a gentle hand on his back. "Just know that I'm here for you."

Diamond went back to her car and began gathering her personal items. But her heart ached for Michael and the pain he was so determined to keep locked up inside.

* * *

"Do you have anything to do right now?" Diamond asked when they were back on the road.

"Not really. Why?"

"I was thinking maybe you could take me by the beach. I've never been to the beach on this side of Florida."

"You want to go swimming?"

"God, no. Only tourists want to go swimming this time of year." She smiled. "I think it's a little too cool for that, but I wouldn't mind walking around for a while. I'm getting used to this peaceful existence in Naples, and I guess I wouldn't mind the opportunity to clear my head. Do some thinking." And she had a feeling Michael could benefit from that, as well.

"All right."

Michael took Diamond on a scenic tour through Naples en route to the beach, pointing out some of the most expensive properties along the way. Diamond was used to dazzling properties where she lived, but some of these were simply magnificent.

"If you ask me, some of these places are overkill," Michael said. "I mean, who needs six bathrooms? Too many of these rich people are so busy making money that they don't spend enough time with their families. They hire nannies, send their kids away to school . . ."

"I hear ya."

Michael parked on a quiet street. Diamond could see the Gulf Coast as she got out of the car. Even from fifty feet away from the beach, she could see that the sand was noticeably whiter on this coast than along the Atlantic.

Noisy seagulls flew overhead. Clearly, they loved the water as much as she did. Why did she rarely head to the ocean in Miami?

Well, she was here now. Smiling, she skipped toward the sand.

She turned to see that Michael was lagging behind her. "Come on, slowpoke," she called.

Michael stood at the walkway that led to the beach. "I've got to take off my running shoes. You're at least wearing sandals."

"Last one to the water buys dinner!" Diamond exclaimed. She scooped up her sandals and took off running. Behind her, she heard Michael call her name in protest, but she didn't stop. She laughed all the way to victory.

"Man, this is cold!" Diamond quickly did a U-turn after her feet hit the water, running back onto the sand. The warm sand stuck to her wet feet.

"C'mon, Michael. You don't know what you're missing."

"I thought you said you wanted to walk. Clear your head."

Diamond went back into the water, forcing herself to adapt to its coldness. "Stop making excuses."

"All right. Here I come." Michael charged toward her, splashing into the water and wetting Diamond in the process. Clearly startled by the water's temperature, he let out a loud cry.

"Hey," Diamond began in a mock stern tone, "watch where those big feet of yours are splashing."

"Pardon me?" Michael kicked water in her direction.

Diamond retaliated, splashing water at Michael with her foot. When he started toward her, she screamed and sprinted away from him. Michael chased her, catching up with her quickly. He wrapped his arms around her waist and lifted her off the ground.

"Michael! Don't, please. I'm sorry." Despite her words, she didn't want him to let her go, because she was very much enjoying the feel of his arms around her.

"Don't what?"

Diamond stilled at the question, picking up on its sexual slant.

"Hmm?" Michael asked, spinning her around to face him. Diamond landed hard against his muscular chest. A frisson of energy passed between them.

She suddenly felt nervous beneath his gaze. She wasn't imagining things. There definitely was some sexual chemistry between them. "You are . . . a big, fat mystery," she said.

He held her tightly, as though he didn't want to let her go. "No one has ever called me fat before."

Diamond giggled. "I didn't say *you* were fat. I said—"

But she couldn't finish her statement. Because Michael's mouth came down on hers, silencing her with a kiss.

CHAPTER TWELVE

Diamond was so surprised by the kiss that all she could do was stand ramrod straight in Michael's arms.

Good Lord, was this actually happening? Michael, who had seemed hell-bent on keeping her at arm's length, was actually kissing her?

Diamond felt as if she were in a dream.

Michael pulled away, saying, "I'm sorry."

Diamond looked up at him for several seconds before speaking. "You kissed me."

"I don't know. I thought I felt something mutual. Maybe it's the beach, the atmosphere. I was wrong, sorry."

He thought she hadn't wanted him to kiss her. Of course, because she hadn't responded. She had just been so startled.

"Michael, it's not that I didn't . . . I feel something, too."

His eyes lit up. "You do?"

"Yes," Diamond admitted on a gush of air. "And it's been frustrating me."

"Me, too."

In the past, Diamond had played games in some of her relationships, or hadn't been completely honest in an attempt to guard her heart. But there was something about Michael that made her want to be totally up front with him.

"I think I was attracted to you the moment I jumped into your car," she said.

"I've been fighting my attraction to you pretty much from that time, as well."

Relieved, Diamond giggled. She reached for his face.

Michael put his hand on hers and slowly removed it. "Diamond, you don't understand."

"What do you mean?"

"I'm attracted to you, but I'm not into casual relationships."

"Let's not jump the gun," Diamond told him. "This is only the beginning."

"But I have to think ahead. I'm attracted to you, but I can't let this go anywhere." He sighed. "I'm not the man I used to be."

"And who was that?"

"A man who was hopeful. A man who had dreams."

"But someone or something took that from you."

"I only wish it was one person or one thing. Maybe I'm scarred, but I'm not ready for anything even remotely resembling a relationship." When Diamond didn't say anything, he went on. "I'm just trying to be honest."

Diamond stepped away from Michael, walking toward the water. His words shouldn't upset her. She barely knew him, and the last thing she should be concerned about was pursuing a relationship. Yet she *was* upset.

"Diamond—"

"No, Michael." She faced him. "You're right. After all, I'm only here for a short time. We need to think with our heads, not anything else."

"I'm glad you understand."

She forced a smile. "What's not to understand? Now, how about we take that walk?"

The next couple of days passed uneventfully. Michael spent a lot of time outside, sanding and painting the exterior of the house. Diamond hung out inside, cleaning the house and otherwise entertaining herself with a video. Sometimes, she walked in the backyard, taking time to think about her past relationships and the various mistakes she had made.

It seemed the one way to convince herself that she needed to concentrate on her future, not on some man.

Not that Michael was merely some man.

It didn't matter. He was off-limits.

Determined to put Michael out of her mind, Diamond padded to the bedroom and retrieved her cell phone. Yesterday, she had called Detective Perez to find out if there had been any sign of Clay. Not that she expected there to be. If Clay knew she was in Naples, he was no doubt hanging around here.

After speaking with the detective and learning nothing helpful, she had called her parents yesterday to fill them in on what was happening. She had also called Tara, but hadn't reached her.

She called her cousin again now.

Tara's husband, Darren, answered on the first ring. "Hello?"

"Hi, Darren. It's me, Diamond."

"Diamond. How are you?"

"I'm doing all right. Keeping a low profile."

"You know Tara's worried out of her mind."

"I know. You got my message yesterday?"

"Yes, but you didn't say much. Then Tara called you back but only got your voice mail."

"I must have been away from my phone. Is Tara home?"

"Let me get her for you."

Seconds later, Tara came to the line. "Hey, Diamond."

"Hi." It was good to hear her cousin's voice.

"Do you know when you're coming home?"

"No," Diamond admitted. "I didn't want to tell you in my message yesterday, but my car was vandalized. I'm sure it was Clay."

"What?"

Diamond explained what had happened.

"If that's the case, Diamond, then you're in more danger staying in Naples. If you can rent a car and head back here, or if we pick you up, Clay will probably think you're still there."

"That idea crossed my mind. But because of the narcotics issue, the police want me to stay around— in case they need to question me further."

"I don't feel good with you being there. You're so far from home. All alone."

"Well," Diamond began, "I'm not exactly alone."

"Oh?"

"I didn't tell you before. But the guy whose car I ran into . . . I'm staying with him."

"You're what?" Tara asked, clearly shocked.

"He's a cop," Diamond quickly explained. "And

I know what you're thinking. Paul's a cop. But this guy, he's nothing like Paul.''

"Diamond, you barely know him."

"And you didn't know Darren when he came into your life and wooed you until you fell in love. But you'd known Harris for five years, only to learn that you didn't know him at all."

"I only want you to be careful."

"I am being careful. In fact, if it wasn't for Michael, Clay may have gotten to me already."

"Michael, huh?"

"Yeah. And he's an interesting character, let me tell you. Apparently he's a cop in Fort Lauderdale, but he's on a leave of absence right now. I've asked him why, but he won't tell me anything. He lives in this small house that seems to be in the middle of nowhere, and I thought I'd hate it, but it's actually growing on me."

There was a pause, then Tara asked, "Is that the only thing growing on you?"

"Huh?"

"You're pretty independent, Diamond. I can't see you staying with Michael unless you want to be there. Unless there's some sort of interest . . ."

Diamond blew out a long breath, then spilled everything. She trusted Tara with even the dumbest things she had done in her life. "He's really hot, Tara. Not that that's the main thing, because I've learned that looks don't count for anything. I tried to deny it and push it aside, but there's definitely an attraction between us. And yesterday—he kissed me."

"My goodness, Diamond."

"I know. It was totally unexpected. He's been hot and cold, and half the time I haven't known what to think. Not that I've been thinking about him a lot, given the Clay situation. Okay, that's not true. I have been thinking about him a lot."

"Sounds like you really like him."

"I do." The admission surprised her. Then she remembered Michael's words a couple of days earlier, and her stomach sank. "But I think it's fairly pointless. He told me that he's not ready for another relationship. I wish he'd tell me about what happened in his past, because I sense a lot of pain, but he won't say a word."

"Maybe he's not ready. I can't believe I'm saying this, but give him some time. If it's meant to be, it'll be. I wasn't ready when Darren came into my life, but now I'm happier than I ever thought possible."

"I know."

"And you were always much more of a romantic that I was."

"I don't want to be a fool, Tara. That's my biggest fear. I haven't made the smartest decisions when it comes to relationships."

"Take it one day at a time. That's all you can do."

"True." Diamond laid her head back on one of the pillows. "The one good thing about being here is that I feel safe. Michael says that Clay won't hurt me while I'm with him, and I believe him."

"Well, I'm glad you're not alone. And I'm glad you're with someone determined to protect you. Where Clay's concerned, you don't know what he's capable of."

Diamond shivered. "I know. Listen, I'll call you again in a couple of days. Maybe I'll even be on my way home by then."

"Please take care of yourself."

"I will. Love you."

"Love you, too. 'Bye."

Diamond sat up when she heard the soft rapping at the bedroom door. She straightened her skirt around her thighs. "Come in."

The door opened, and Michael peeked his head inside. "You sleeping?"

"No. I was reading."

"You hungry?"

She nodded.

"Good. I was thinking maybe you wanted to cook dinner tonight?"

"I could . . . but you'd have to eat it at your own risk." She smiled sweetly.

"Naw, I'm kidding. I learned my lesson after the eggs. But I was thinking you might be tired of my cooking. Want to head out somewhere for dinner?"

Diamond shrugged. "If you want to."

"Great. Can you be ready in twenty minutes?"

Diamond got to her feet. "Sure."

As soon as Michael closed the door, Diamond headed to her suitcase. She searched the contents for something suitable to wear. Her strappy orange sandals were in there. She lifted one, wondering if she should wear the new dress she had bought. Michael had really liked that dress. But if she wore it, would he think she was wearing it for him?

Diamond decided on a floral sundress that came to just above her knees. But as she stood in front of the mirror, she frowned. It was a simple dress, but also very flattering. It accentuated her narrow waist and full hips. Michael could just as easily think she was hoping to intrigue him wearing this dress.

Diamond groaned. Why was she giving a second thought to what Michael might construe? Normally, she would put this dress on without a second thought.

She took another look at herself in the mirror and decided she looked good. If Michael couldn't deal with it, too bad.

"So," Diamond began, "where are we going?"

"To Island Delights. It's a quaint little restaurant that features Caribbean cuisine. I discovered it around three months ago, and since that time, it's become my favorite spot in Naples."

"I love Caribbean food."

"I'm glad to hear it. This one is owned by a Jamaican family, so if you like spicy jerk pork and curried chicken, this will be right up your alley."

"I do."

They drove in silence for several minutes. Michael glanced Diamond's way more than once, and each time, she was staring out the window.

He let his gaze fall to her legs. One beautiful leg was crossed over the other, causing her skirt to crawl way up her thigh. His heart nearly stopped. She was, quite simply, beautiful. *Breathtaking*. She had curves in all the right places, curves it was hard for a man not to notice.

Michael had the feeling that Diamond could make a paper bag look enticing.

Somehow, they had managed to stay out of each other's way for the most part over the past two days. He felt bad about the kiss and about how he had pushed her away afterward. But he hadn't been able to keep her out of his thoughts and his dreams.

It would be so much easier if she went away,

disappeared as quickly as she had come into his life. No, that wasn't true. If Diamond left now, Michael knew he would think about her for a very long time.

Think about her, then forget about her.

It would have to be that way.

So why did something in his gut tell him Diamond was not the type of woman he could easily forget?

"What are you thinking?" he asked.

She turned to face him, slipping one leg off the other as she did. "Nothing. Just taking in the view."

"What perfume are you wearing?" he asked. "That's a pretty fragrance."

"Oh. Thanks. Actually, it's a natural oil I picked up at a shop in Miami. I don't know what it's called."

"It really suits you."

Diamond flashed him a soft smile, then once again faced the window.

He knew what she was thinking. That he was one big contradiction. Kissing her, then pushing her away, then complimenting her.

And she was right. He needed to make up his mind. Either he wanted to be with her, or he didn't.

CHAPTER THIRTEEN

Island Delights was packed. Diamond thought they would have to wait for a table with the rest of the hungry people in the line, but to her pleasant surprise, Michael had reserved a table so they were able to be seated right away.

The waitress who led them to their table for two was dressed in a white tank top and brightly colored floral skirt. It reminded Diamond of something she'd seen in pictures and commercials promoting travel to the Caribbean.

To the left of their table was a fake cascading waterfall, but the water was quite real. The waterfall ran into a small stream that seemed to border the length of the restaurant. A large palm tree stood in the center of the two-level establishment, and several other vibrant green plants were strategically placed to give the feel of actually being on an island. Pure white sand even surrounded the base of the palm tree.

"This is gorgeous," Diamond announced as she

turned to face Michael. "I can't believe the elaborate setup."

"I fell in love with it the first time I saw it."

Averting her gaze to the far left of the restaurant, she saw a medium-sized dark stage, dimly lit with various small colored bulbs—the kind of bulbs one would find on a Christmas tree. "Do they actually have live entertainment here?" she asked, noting the soft sounds of island reggae coming from the speakers above.

Michael nodded. "It's a bit early still. The band usually arrives around eight-thirty."

"Evening." The arrival of their waiter drew their gazes to him. "What can I get you to drink?"

Looking at Diamond, Michael shrugged. "What would you like?"

"A piña colada. Nice and creamy, please."

"I'll have a Coke," Michael said.

Diamond narrowed her eyes at him. "Doesn't a place like this make you want to have a tropical drink?"

"Coke," Michael repeated to the waiter. As the waiter walked away, he said to Diamond, "I'm not really a drinker."

"Really?"

"Really."

"You mean you never drink?"

"Not anymore."

He offered no other explanation, but once again, Diamond was intrigued by what he hadn't said. Of course, she was inquisitive by nature, and could very well be looking for some big story where there was none.

Michael glanced around, then turned his attention back to Diamond. His dark eyes were soft, yet seemed to have some magnetic quality. They drew her in, beguiling her.

"Why are you looking at me like that?" he asked.

Michael's smooth, deep voice caused an electrical current to flow through her blood. "Like what?"

"Eyes narrowed. Like you're trying to figure me out."

"Maybe I am."

Michael shifted in his seat. "I know you're used to asking people questions, but I have one for you."

"Okay."

"Is Diamond your real name?"

She couldn't help laughing. "Why do you ask?"

"I don't know. Diamond sounds like a stage name."

"It's officially my name now, but my parents didn't give it to me. I was born Karen Elizabeth Montgomery. Bo-ring. As a child, people started to call me Diamond because of my eyes. My mother said they sparkled like diamonds. The nickname stuck, and four years ago, I legally changed my name to add Diamond to the beginning."

"I see. Where are your parents?"

"In Broward."

"Any brothers or sisters?"

"One sister. Older. She lives in New Orleans. What about you? Any sisters or brothers?"

"I have one sister as well. Lives in the Fort Lauderdale area. She's four years younger than me."

"How old are you?"

"Thirty-two. You?"

"Twenty-seven." She paused. "Any brothers?"

Michael shook his head. "No brothers."

"What about your parents?"

Michael's face grew grim. "They died in a house fire eight years ago."

"Oh, my God." Diamond wanted to reach out and stroke his face, to make the hurt she saw in his beautiful brown eyes go away. She didn't. Instead she said, "I'm sorry."

"I get a bit of comfort from the fact that they were together in the end. After that, it was just me and my sister. We have some relatives in Toronto, where we were raised, and we see them once in a while."

Diamond rested her chin on her linked fingers. "You grew up in Toronto?"

"Mmm-hmm. Until my father's company opened up an office down here and offered him the chance to move. He always loved the warm weather, and jumped at the chance."

"What's Toronto like?"

"Really nice. Pretty multicultural. I'm sure you'd like it."

The waiter arrived with their drinks and announced that he would be back in a few minutes to take their orders. Diamond took a sip of the piña colada, pleasantly surprised that it was exactly the way she liked them. Stirring her drink with her straw, she asked, "Do you miss it?"

Michael took a sip of his soda. "In a way. But I certainly don't miss the winters."

"I'd like to go there one day," Diamond announced. "I'd like to go to a lot of places. My cousin is a travel agent, and she's gotten to go on some neat trips."

"But you work a lot, don't you?"

"Yeah, I do. And that keeps me pretty much rooted in Miami. But I can't let my entire life pass me by without experiencing what the world has to offer.''

Michael had felt that way too, once. Now, he didn't believe the world necessarily had anything to offer other than trials and heartache. He didn't say that, though.

''You've suffered a lot of pain in your life, haven't you, Michael?''

Michael's eyes flew to Diamond's at the question. It surprised him. ''Wait a second. One minute we're talking about traveling, and then you ask me a question like that?''

''Am I wrong?''

Michael didn't respond.

''I don't know. I'm sitting here looking at you, and I see pain in your eyes. Pain and fear.''

Michael groaned. ''C'mon, Diamond. You're not going to start that again.''

''I wish you'd open up to me.''

''Why?'' Michael challenged.

Because I care about you! Diamond wanted to retort, but she couldn't find the courage to say the words. ''I . . . appreciate how you've been helping me. I want to return the favor.''

''Everyone's had heartache. Everyone's had a relationship that didn't work out. Right?''

''Yes.''

''So why don't you tell me about him?''

''All right. Well, there were several. Not that many,'' she quickly amended, not wanting Michael to get the wrong idea. ''But enough to make me realize that I totally suck at the love game.''

''Keep talking.''

''My ex was a cop. But he's almost as unstable as Clay. He wanted so badly to control me, he became a stalker, trying to make me believe someone was out to hurt me.''

"You're kidding?"

"I wish I was. It's a long, convoluted story, and that's the gist of it. Then there was Tyrone. We were engaged—until I found out he was cheating on me.''

"He cheated on a woman like you?"

Diamond's breath snagged at Michael's indirect compliment. "Some guys don't know how good they have it, I guess.''

"I guess."

Her eyes locking on his, Diamond stared at Michael. Damn, but the man was so hard to read. Should she take his words as flirtation, or was he simply being kind?

The waiter returned then, and Diamond ordered the curried chicken dinner. So did Michael.

"So what do you do out here in Naples?" Diamond asked, bringing the subject back to him.

"Not much."

"And when do you think you'll head back to Fort Lauderdale? To work?"

"I'm not sure."

Something was going on there. Diamond knew it. Something he was running from. But how could she get him to open up?

If she had been making any headway, it was all for naught. The lights dimmed, and a round of applause filled the air. Diamond and Michael looked up to see that the band had arrived.

So much for getting to know him better.

The music was intoxicating, and even though they had finished eating, Diamond and Michael stayed at their table, swaying to the various reggae beats. With a bit of envy, Diamond watched couples dance on the floor, and wished that Michael's arms were wrapped around her right now.

What would she tell one of her callers? She'd tell her to go for it, not let fear hold her back.

Aided by the courage that often came from alcohol, Diamond pushed back her seat and stood. She reached for Michael's hand and tugged on it. "Let's dance."

Michael's eyes bulged, as if she had asked him to do something dangerous, like jump off a very tall building. "Dance?"

"Yeah." She moved her body erotically in front of him. "Isn't the music moving you?"

"I'm enjoying it from right here."

"C'mon. Don't be a sore sport."

Around them, Diamond heard a few people say, "Dance with the lady," and "I wish I had someone as beautiful as her to dance with." She pulled Michael's hand once more, and this time, he stood.

She led him to the dance floor, swaying her hips to the music as she did. The band was performing a mellow Bob Marley tune.

"I'm not the world's best dancer," Michael warned her.

"With a body like yours, I doubt that." She ran her fingers down Michael's chest. "Show me what you've got."

Michael looked down at her with a confused expression.

"Are you all right?"

" '. . . and feel all right . . .' " she sang in her best imitation of Bob Marley singing "One Love." Then she grinned at Michael. "Oh, yeah, I'm definitely all right."

She's tipsy, Michael thought, smiling wryly. *And flirtatious.*

A dangerous combination.

"Hold me, Michael." Diamond draped her arms around his neck.

Resigned to his fate, he slipped his arms around her waist and pulled her close.

Diamond shouldn't have had that third piña colada. Michael was doing his best to resist her, but it was going to be damn near impossible if she was all over him.

"You have a great body," Diamond said. She giggled. "Did I say that already?"

Diamond pressed her body closer to his, and Michael ran his hands down her back to the groove right above her buttocks. All he had to do was lower his palms and he would see for himself if her butt felt as nice as it looked.

"You've got a pretty amazing body yourself," Michael told her.

"Just not amazing enough."

"Hmm?" Michael pulled back to look down at her. "Why would you say that?"

" 'Cause you don't like being near me. You can't wait for me to leave."

She was more than tipsy. Now slightly slurring her words, Michael knew she was drunk. Even if she hadn't been slurring her words, it was clear that the alcohol had loosened her tongue. Michael doubted she would say what she was saying if sober.

"That's not true. I don't want you to leave."

Diamond sighed happily and dropped her head against his chest. She was soft and warm, and man, did she ever feel good. Michael had almost forgotten what it felt like to hold a woman in his arms.

They continued dancing even as the songs

changed. Michael was holding her closer now, bending his head so that his chin rested on the top of her hair. He wanted to do more than hold her. He wanted to kiss her again. She had the most incredible soft lips, and he couldn't help wanting to sample them again. He couldn't help wondering how her lips and tongue would feel skimming his chest and other parts of his body.

He was so tempted. And he knew she would kiss him back, unlike the first time. Like a moth to a flame, he was inexplicably drawn to her and he didn't want to pull away.

"I like how you hold me, Michael. So strong."

Lord help him. "I like it, too."

"I want you to hold me like this all night."

Her words conjured a quick vision of the two of them naked in his bed, Diamond on top of him as they made love.

Diamond was fire and passion and a man would have to be dead to not want to experience being with her.

"You say that now," Michael began, "but I doubt you'll feel the same way in the morning."

"Huh-uh." She giggled.

The song ended, and as hard as it was, Michael pulled away from her. She looked up at him with hazy eyes.

"I think we should go," he told her.

A slow smile spread on her face. "Hmm."

Man, oh, man. He couldn't bring her home. Not when it was clear she had thoughts of doing the nasty with him.

"Yeah. Maybe take a walk on the beach. Sober up."

She poked a finger into his chest. "I knew you didn't like me."

Michael took her hand in his and led her back to their table. "I'm not even gonna go there."

"I don't really feel like going for a walk. Can't we just go home?"

Home. The word conjured memories of the life he had shared with Debra and Ashley. A life that had been taken away from him.

Could he have a life with Diamond?

"Please . . ."

Michael retrieved her purse from the chair and returned to her just as she faltered a little. He quickly put an arm around her waist to steady her.

"All right, Diamond. We'll go home."

Michael had the feeling this was going to be one long, hot, and bothered night.

CHAPTER FOURTEEN

Diamond's eyes flew open in the darkness. Instantly, she had the distinct sense that something was wrong.

She lay very still, thinking. And then it hit her. Hadn't she been out at dinner with Michael? Yes, she had. So how was it that she was now in his bed, waking up from sleep?

Slowly, Diamond sat up. She stifled a yawn. In the dark room, she couldn't see the clock behind her, but it had to be the middle of the night.

She was missing a big chunk of time. They had had a lovely dinner, the band had started to play. She'd had a few drinks . . .

Diamond had a fuzzy memory of dancing with Michael, but she wasn't sure if it was really a memory or a dream.

Oh, no. She gently squeezed her forehead. Had she made a fool of herself? She wouldn't doubt it, especially since she didn't remember leaving the restaurant or heading back here, and she certainly didn't remember getting into bed.

Throwing the covers off, Diamond swung her feet over the side of the bed. She was still wearing her floral dress, so she *had* been out cold when returning to the house. But what was the memory flitting in and out of her brain too quickly to grasp?

She forced herself to think harder, and moments later, her heart dropped to the pit of her stomach. It was really hazy, but she could almost picture not wanting to let go of Michael as he had placed her on the bed. She could see herself kissing his lips, his chin. And he was . . . he was trying to pry her hands from around his neck.

Diamond groaned loudly. If that was a memory— and she couldn't see it not being one—then she had indeed made a fool of herself.

Not being a big drinker, she normally preferred a glass of wine or a wine cooler to stronger drinks. But she'd had, what—two piña coladas? No, she distinctly remembered finishing the second one and quickly ordering a third.

She didn't remember anything after that.

At least she would be able to blame any out-of-character behavior on the alcohol.

Michael was a gentleman; she didn't doubt that for a minute. But if she *had* thrown herself at him, had he been tempted? Or offended?

Maybe he had simply been embarrassed for her.

Then again, maybe he *had* been tempted . . .

Diamond stood and stretched, then looked over her shoulder at the bed. There was something about that spacious bed that made her feel uneasy.

Or hot and bothered.

She wrapped her arms around her torso. Michael's alluring masculine scent was everywhere. It lingered in the pillows and sheets, even though he had changed them for her. It seemed to ooze from the walls. It was almost like a living entity, one that followed her everywhere.

No wonder it was hard to get him out of her system.

Diamond wandered to the window. She slipped her fingers between the blinds, peering outside.

And got the shock of her life.

Michael, his body wet and glistening beneath the moonlight, was climbing out of the pool.

Naked as the day he had been born.

Diamond pulled her hands from the blinds as if she had been zapped by electricity. Then she stood still in the darkness, not even breathing for several seconds.

She counted to ten. Told herself to go to back to bed. She was thirsty, but she wouldn't die without a drink of water before the morning. Right now, it was crucial that she didn't alert Michael to the fact that she was awake, that she had been looking at him. All she had to do was walk the few feet back to the bed . . .

She stepped up to the window and once again peered through the blinds.

My, oh, my. She had thought Michael gorgeous before, but he looked absolutely magnificent now. He had the firmest butt she had ever seen on a man. And a very strong, muscularly defined back.

Oh, like she cared about his back!

Turn around, turn around. . . .

She felt a flush of heat at her thoughts and couldn't help swallowing. Then came the stab of guilt. She was acting like a pervert, for goodness' sake!

This was Michael's place and he was fully entitled to swim in the nude if that's what he wanted to do. And he was entitled to do it in privacy.

Yet Diamond couldn't tear her eyes away.

Michael walked several feet around the edge of the pool, his back still to her. He stopped, stretched his hands high above his head, then dove in. Water splashed into the air, looking like beads of floating crystal beneath the moonlight.

He swam half the length of the large pool with his entire body underwater. When he finally burst to the surface, he was facing the bedroom window.

Startled, Diamond edged her body back and narrowed the opening between the blinds. He couldn't see her, could he?

He continued to stare in her direction, then maneuvered himself onto his back and began swimming to the pool's far end.

With his gaze no longer in her direction, Diamond finally stepped back from the window. She walked the few feet to Michael's bed and lowered her body onto its edge, releasing a shaky breath as she did.

Her body was throbbing just from looking at him. Diamond appreciated an attractive man just like the next woman, but she couldn't ever remember feeling hot and bothered just from looking at one the way she did now that she had spent a few minutes checking out Michael. And she had seen some fine brothers at more than one strip club, men whose physiques were top-notch.

Yet she hadn't lusted over them. Michael, she had.

Still was.

Diamond lay on her side, curling her body into a ball. How could she continue to stay here? She had never been so damn sexually frustrated in all her life, and she didn't like feeling this way. But worse was the niggling thought that what she felt for Michael was more than just a physical attraction.

When had her feelings for him grown? Thinking the situation over, she could only conclude that it had happened in a heartbeat.

One minute, she was worried about Clay and if or when he would be caught. The next, she was falling for the mysterious, brooding, incredibly handsome Michael.

Of all the people to fall for, a man who pretty much told you that he could never give you his heart ought to be on the bottom of any woman's list.

Ought to be.

Lord help her, she was in big trouble. She had sensed it from day one, which was why she had wanted to get back on the road as soon as possible. Maybe her car would be ready within hours and she could thank Michael for helping her out, then take off. Maybe it wasn't too late for her heart.

But how could she leave him? At dinner, they had made some headway, talking about their lives. She had seen the pain and fear in his eyes, and she had felt the strongest pull to help make his pain go away.

Yes, she had a life to get back to, but that didn't seem to matter now. Michael was all she could think about.

A memory from high school flooded her mind. James Hinze had been an oxymoron—drop-dead gorgeous, star football player, but quiet and brooding. He dazzled everyone with his quarterback skills and seemed like he would be the most outgoing guy, but whenever there was a party thrown by the football team, he never showed.

Diamond had gotten to know him in her senior

English class. And while many women had been attracted to James for his good looks and athletic ability—the talk was that he'd definitely make pro one day—Diamond had been attracted to him for another reason. She had first been drawn to him because of the element of intrigue that surrounded him. She wanted to get to know what made him tick, what he was really like beneath the limited bit he showed the public.

That had ultimately led to them talking and becoming friends. Diamond had a way of making him open up to her. She had discovered that James had grown up with an overbearing father and had learned to keep his emotions inside. And despite his excellent sports ability, at his core he was insecure and felt mostly unloved—a fact that surely would have shocked all his fans. And while some guys would be extremely flattered by everyone telling them how great they were, James wasn't interested in people who were attracted to him for what they saw on the surface. As a result, some people had seen him as a snob, when the truth was, they hadn't understood him.

Diamond had been able to draw him out of his shell—to make him smile. And eventually, she had been able to make him open up to the possibility of love.

When James had been killed in an automobile accident, Diamond had been devastated. He had been her first love, and after his death, she never thought she would love again.

Such a long time ago, she thought, feeling nostalgic.

She remembered the men who had followed James. She hadn't put two and two together before, but now that she thought about it, practically every relationship since James had been about finding that special connection. She would rush headlong into a relationship after an initial attraction, only to find out the man wasn't what she wanted. However, three years ago when she had met Tyrone, the sparks had been intense—sparks she didn't figure would ever die. Tyrone was a father, who had two children from a previous relationship, which was fine by her. And when he had proposed to her within a year of their relationship, Diamond had happily accepted.

But once again, her heart had been broken. Unlike James, Tyrone didn't die. He cheated on her with his ex—time and time again. Diamond had suspected something was wrong, and Tyrone finally admitted to her that he still had feelings for his ex-girlfriend and therefore didn't know if their marriage would work out.

She had kicked him out of her life and her apartment, and made the decision to harden herself to love.

There had been a few men since Tyrone, but Diamond had been able to keep her promise to herself. She had never given them her heart. At the first sign of trouble, she bolted. Because Paul had seemed very decent, she had made an exception and moved in, but still, she had held back—something he had sensed. While there was no excuse for what he had done, the fact that she hadn't been able to love him completely was no doubt the catalyst for his actions.

Her trip down memory lane was making one thing clear to her. Getting involved with Michael would be a very bad thing. Maybe she'd be better off dating a guy for two years before taking any step toward a real relationship.

And if you can hold out for two years, then that would be a relationship with zero passion. Which would totally depress her. Passion was the last thing Diamond wanted to live without.

Enough thinking already, she told herself. As it was, she would probably have a headache in the morning, given that she'd had too much to drink.

She was pulling the covers around her when she heard the knock on her bedroom door. Her pulse took off running at a record-breaking speed. Why was Michael knocking on the door at this hour?

Should she respond? Should she quickly lie back and pretend she was sleeping?

There was another knock.

"Uh . . . yeah?"

The door slowly opened. "You are up."

Diamond stared at Michael in the room's shadows. Her Adonis, clad only in shorts, looked powerful and tantalizing.

"Something wrong?" she asked.

"I thought I saw you at the window while I was swimming."

Damn, so he *had* spotted her. "Sorry, Michael. I was restless, got up . . . I didn't know you'd be out there."

He strolled slowly into the room, and with each step closer seemed to steal more and more of her breath. Diamond's heart was throbbing so loudly, she was sure he could hear it echoing off the walls.

"Are you all right?" he asked.

"All right?" Diamond repeated, not understanding what he meant.

"You had a few drinks. You were pretty out of it."

"Oh." She moaned her embarrassment. "Look, I'm really sorry if—"

But Michael was lowering himself onto the bed, slowly edging closer to her, snaking his arm around her waist.

Then all Diamond's thoughts turned to mush as Michael closed the distance between them and covered her lips with his.

CHAPTER FIFTEEN

Michael was kissing her again! And like the first time, Diamond simply stayed there, immobile, not sure what to do. Not sure this was really happening.

Not sure if she remembered how to breathe . . .

This time, Michael didn't pull away. Gently, he began to move his lips over hers, coaxing any fear out of her body. With a sigh of surrender, Diamond melted against him and began to kiss him back with all the passion she had kept locked up inside.

Michael wrapped both arms around her. Diamond slipped her arms around his neck. Her breasts pressed against his hard, naked chest, and she wished she were naked, too.

"Diamond, I swear. You do something to me every time I look at you. Touching you . . . God, I can't get enough."

Her head spinning, Diamond held on to him tighter. She opened her mouth wide, allowing Michael's tongue deep inside her. He sucked and nipped. She did the same, feeling all the while that this wasn't enough. The kiss electrified every part of her, but made her want even more.

Diamond kneaded her fingers down his muscular back. A low, sexy growl emanated from Michael's chest, and suddenly he had his arms all over her body, caressing her back, sliding his hands beneath her dress and onto her thighs.

"I want you out of this," Michael rasped.

"Take it off me."

They continued to kiss each other even as they moved to a standing position. Even as Diamond lifted her arms up so that Michael could slip her dress over her head. Their lips separated only briefly then, and Michael tossed the sundress onto the floor.

Michael scooped Diamond into his arms in one swift motion. They were both topless now, and her breasts pressed against his hard torso. "Wrap your legs around me, Diamond."

She did, then trailed her tongue from his ear to the tip of his chin.

"You drive me crazy, you know that?" Michael's breath was hot against her ear. "You've been driving me crazy since the first time I laid eyes on you. I want to make love to you so badly—"

"Oh, Michael." Diamond could hardly breathe, she was so excited. She dug her fingers into his back. "I can't wait to make love to you."

He carried her the short distance to the bed and laid her down. He removed her panties at a frantic pace, then kissed her hungrily, making her body come alive with the most overpowering desire she had ever felt. Never had she wanted to make love so badly. Diamond grabbed at his shorts, needing him to be free of them. She dragged them over his taut behind and strong thighs.

Now naked beside her, Michael slowed the pace. He trailed gentle fingers down the front of her body. "You're perfect." He ran a finger up again and stroked circles around her nipple. "So beautiful."

The next moment, his mouth was on her breast, his hot tongue on her nipple. Instantly, it grew taut in his mouth. The core of her body throbbed in response, the sweet sensations almost overwhelming her. She palmed his head, held it close to her as he suckled one breast, then the other.

Diamond looked down at him, at his hungry mouth on her breast, thinking the sight was the most erotically beautiful thing in the world. Finally, her eyes fluttering shut, she threw her head back, arching into him as the pressure inside her built. She was panting and moaning so hard, she hardly recognized the sounds as coming from her lips.

If Michael kept up this exquisite torture, she would explode at any moment. "Do you have a condom?" she asked.

"Yeah." Michael reached for the night table and opened the drawer. He fumbled around. Diamond heard the sound of a package tearing.

"Let me do it." Diamond took the condom from him and positioned herself over his body. Slowly, she rolled it over his erection.

As soon as she was done, Michael took her upper arms in his, pulled her toward him, and locked lips with hers. His tongue twisting with hers, he maneuvered her onto her side, then got on top of her. He slipped his hands between her legs and moaned hotly into her ear when he found her slick and ready. Then, with one powerful thrust, he entered her.

Diamond cried out and dug her fingers into his

skin. He wasn't gentle; instead he loved her like a man starved. It was wild and crazy, a side to Michael that surprised her at the same time that it thrilled her. Together, they moved to a frenzied rhythm that proved their coupling had been inevitable.

As a familiar tightening began in her center, Diamond gripped Michael's buttocks. Two more deep strokes and she exploded into a million pieces. "Michael!" she cried, holding him tight as wave after dizzying wave of contractions rocked her body.

He didn't slow his pace, but rather thrust harder, held her tighter. Moments later, he let out a loud moan as he succumbed to his own release.

Finally, Michael eased his slick body off of Diamond's. He shifted himself until he was beside her on the bed. He reached for her, and she nestled herself in his arms.

"Michael—"

"Shh." He placed a finger on her lips. "No talk, okay?"

Diamond kissed his chest. "Okay."

Later that night, Michael lay awake, listening to the quiet of the night and the steady sound of Diamond's breathing.

He had made love to her. And it had been the most amazing lovemaking he had ever experienced.

His hunger for her had surprised him. He couldn't remember ever such a wild and frenzied coupling in his life. But not only had he come away physically satisfied, he felt like the emotional void inside him wasn't quite as vast anymore.

Michael wasn't yet ready to think about tomorrow, but he felt a measure of hope he hadn't felt in a while.

It was a nice feeling.

"Are you gonna be all right here by yourself for a little while?" Michael asked Diamond. Dressed only in a pair of boxers, he was freshly showered, and beads of moisture clung to his hair.

She sat up in the bed, pulling the sheet around her. "Yeah. Why?"

"I have a few errands to run. I want to check my post office box and maybe pick up a few groceries." He winked. "Some more eggs."

"Sure. I'll take a shower, and if you're not back by the time I'm done, I'll have some toast."

"All right." He leaned across the bed and kissed her softly on the lips. "I'll see you later."

Michael flashed her a smile when he was at the bedroom door. Diamond wiggled her fingers at him; then he disappeared.

Lying back, she sighed happily. Last night had been incredible—intense in a way she hadn't anticipated.

Right now, she didn't care about getting her car back. She wanted to stay here in this secluded spot with Michael as long as possible. She wanted to see where this could lead.

Because, to her surprise, she was happy. Happier than she had been in a very long time.

When Diamond heard the knocking at the front door, she rolled her eyes and smiled. Michael must have forgotten his key. This was already feeling domestic, but she didn't mind.

"Coming," she called. Wearing Michael's robe, she ran down the hall and swung the door open. But the smile on her lips died the moment she saw who was there.

It wasn't Michael. It was a woman. A very pretty woman. She wore her hair in long, thin braids that hung well down her back.

Diamond felt a stab of jealousy.

The woman arched an eyebrow and asked, "Who are you?"

Diamond pulled the robe tighter around her. "Who are *you?*"

They stared at each other, clearly assessing the situation. Diamond's stomach felt as if someone had reached inside and squeezed it—hard.

After what seemed like forever, the other woman extended a hand. "I'm Kelly."

Kelly. Diamond tried to swallow her disappointment, but it got stuck in her throat. For Kelly to be here meant she knew Michael. It was highly unlikely that she had taken a wrong turn into this driveway.

Was this Michael's lover? Diamond shifted uncomfortably from one foot to another. If she *was* Michael's lover, did that mean Diamond didn't have a right to feel jealousy? After all, Diamond would be "the other woman" in this situation, something she had never wanted to be in her life. Regardless, she did have a right to feel disillusioned, because it certainly seemed like Michael had lied to her.

Diamond finally took the woman's hand in hers and shook it. "I'm Diamond. And, uh, I know how this must look—"

"You don't have to explain anything."

"No, I think I do. For the record—"

Kelly waved her hands, stopping Diamond. "Whatever you and Michael do is your business. He doesn't have to report to me."

Diamond eyed the woman warily. What did that mean? Did Kelly and Michael have an open relationship, or—

"My brother's probably going to have a fit, thinking I've come to check up on him now. Which, quite frankly, is the truth."

"Your brother?"

Kelly nodded. "Michael says I'm always meddling in his life, but I only want to see him happy. Is he here?"

"Oh, sorry." Diamond stepped back. "No, he's not here right now. I don't think he should be much longer. He's not expecting you?"

"No. I figured I'd surprise him." Kelly gave Diamond a quick once-over. She smirked. "You're wearing his robe."

"I know. I had a shower, and—"

"It's not what it looks like, right?" Kelly chuckled. "Goodness, don't mind me. I always seem to put my foot in my mouth. I told you it was none of my business, and I meant that."

Diamond smiled sweetly, thankful she didn't have to hedge her way out of answering the question.

"Diamond, you said?"

"Uh-huh."

"Maybe you can tell me how you met my brother. I don't think that will be crossing any lines."

"It's a long story," Diamond replied.

Kelly slipped out of her sandals. "I've got time."

* * *

Michael paused at the door when he heard the sound of laughter floating in the air. What the—?

It wasn't the television. That was live laughter—two sets of it. Who was here?

He stepped cautiously into the house. He kept walking until he was right outside the living room, where the laughter was coming from.

Rounding the corner, Michael was shocked to see Diamond and his sister sitting on the sofa. Diamond sat cross-legged facing Kelly. They looked as comfortable as two old friends.

Noticing him, Kelly's laughter faded. "Michael. You didn't tell me you had a celebrity staying with you!"

"Celebrity?"

"Good grief, you're so out of the loop. Lady D of *The Love Chronicles*. She's only the hottest talk radio show host in all of South Florida."

"Oh, you're too kind," Diamond said. But her grin said she was eating up the compliment like a warm biscuit with butter.

As Michael walked farther into the living room, Kelly jumped to her feet. She hurried to him and enveloped him in an enthusiastic hug.

Michael pulled away first. "Why didn't you tell me you were coming, Kelly?"

"You didn't return my calls. I figured you were mad at me, so I decided to come out here to make amends."

"You should have left me a message." Not that it would have done much good. Michael had turned the ringers off the phones, and he hadn't bothered to check his voice mail.

"I'm sorry. I didn't mean to intrude. But you know how worried I've been about you." She glanced over her shoulder at Diamond, who was now standing. "And I'm glad I did. Because if I hadn't, I wouldn't have met the infamous Lady D."

"Excuse us a minute, Diamond?" Michael said.

"Sure."

He wrapped his fingers around Kelly's wrist and walked with her into the hallway. Once they were several feet away from the living room, he said, "You know I don't like surprises."

"And you know I don't like worrying sick about you."

"Maybe you wouldn't have to worry if I felt you weren't trying to pry. Is that what this visit is about? You coming here to spy on me?"

"Oh, don't be so dramatic."

"You never come out here," Michael pointed out.

"There's a first time for everything. Please don't be mad, Michael."

Man, his sister was going to drive him nuts one of these days. But he knew that as stubborn and tunnel-visioned as she was, she did care about him. And it had always been hard to stay mad at her when she pleaded with him in that soft, vulnerable voice of hers. "I'm not mad."

A grin broke out on her face. "Good."

"But that doesn't mean I want you to make a habit of this."

"I understand."

Michael drew in a deep breath. "What did you tell her?"

"Tell her about what?"

"About me?"

"Nothing. Well, only that I thought you were mad at me, but I didn't get into why."

"You didn't tell her about Ashley?" he asked, not ready to fully relax.

"No."

"Debra?"

"No. I was telling her about my various boyfriends, and all the bad luck I've had finding Mr. Right. She had some great advice for me." Kelly had shared with Diamond the truth that the one guy she'd loved in high school still had her heart—sexy Ashton Hunter—even though he had taken her virginity and then taken off.

"Good. I don't want her to know anything about Ashley or Debra."

Kelly sighed. "Michael, do you still think it's good to keep this all in? Ashley and Debra were a part of your life. Denying them—"

"I'm not denying them."

"Then what can it hurt to talk about them? That's what Diamond does. She talks to people about their problems."

"She's a radio personality, not a psychiatrist."

"And she's also very perceptive, and very compassionate."

"You heard what I said."

The firm set of Michael's jaw told Kelly there was no point in continuing this conversation. "All right. You know how I feel, but I won't press the issue."

"Thank you."

Kelly paused, glanced around. "How long will she be staying?"

"I'm not sure."

"Oh?"

"Did she tell you what's going on?"

"You mean between the two of you?"

"No." Michael leveled a hard gaze on his sister.

He never discussed his love life with her. Not that he'd had one since Debra, anyway. "About the guy—"

"Oh, yeah. The psycho who's after her."

"Yeah."

"Uh-huh. What a freaky story! I swear, sometimes it doesn't pay to be famous."

Michael ignored his sister's comment, saying, "Given what's going on, I'm not sure when she'll head home. Her car still needs work. And at least . . . at least she's safe here."

"Hmm. So you care."

"I do have a heart, Kelly."

"Are you sure that's all there is to this?"

"Why . . . what did she say?"

"Oh, don't go stressing yourself. Diamond's apparently as secretive as you. She won't tell me anything, though she was wearing your robe earlier." One perfectly sculpted eyebrow lifted suggestively.

"She probably had a shower."

Kelly frowned. "That's what she said."

"See?"

Kelly rolled her eyes, though she smiled. Michael was entirely too smug. But he was still her brother, and she knew him better than he thought she did. "Well, no one could blame you for getting involved with Diamond. She's beautiful, smart, famous . . . And you're still a man."

"I'm also a cop who doesn't want to see anything bad happen to anyone. As soon as this is all resolved, Diamond will head back to Miami. And I'll be staying here."

Once again, Michael was putting an end to a conversation without giving her the answers she craved. But his body language had changed, and

Kelly would swear that he had feelings for Diamond.

Even if he didn't want to admit it.

Change of plans.

With each passing day, Clay grew angrier and more frustrated. He had hoped to see Diamond return to the auto shop to pick up her car, but so far she hadn't.

He wanted to believe that she had headed back to Miami, but something in his gut told him she was still here, still hanging with that guy. And that made him angry.

He was staying in a different cheap motel every night, just in case the witch had the cops looking for him. At least they didn't know what kind of car he was driving. At night, he dreamed of what he would do to her. Sometimes, he imagined having hot, dirty sex with her, then strangling the life out of her. Other times, he imagined punishing her first, then doing what he wanted to her lifeless body.

The fantasies kept him going.

But last night, he had realized that he wasn't going to be able to get close to her here. Not while she was staying with that guy.

He needed to get her back to Miami. He needed to get her alone.

Then he would act out one of his fantasies.

Vengeance *would* be his.

CHAPTER SIXTEEN

"Are you sure you have to go?" Diamond asked Kelly.

She nodded. "Yeah. I'd better hit the road. I don't normally like to drive in the dark, and it's getting fairly late."

Diamond hugged her new friend. They had enjoyed many laughs over several hours, for which Diamond was grateful. "It was great to meet you."

"Are you kidding?" Kelly's eyes bulged. "Meeting you was a definite dream. I mean, who would have thought I'd run into Lady D at my brother's place? My friends will be so envious."

Diamond smiled. "You have my number. Let's stay in touch."

"Definitely. And I'm gonna try and take your advice."

"If it works for you, it works. If it doesn't, it doesn't. Truly, I'm no expert."

"Oh, sure."

"Be careful, sis." Michael stepped forward and

gave Kelly a warm hug, then released her. "Now that you know I'm okay, next time call first."

"I will. But don't be a stranger."

"I will try to be better about staying in touch."

"Wow," Kelly said, feigning surprise. "You know, Diamond, I think you're good for my brother."

Michael flashed his sister a wry smile. "I thought you said you wanted to hit the road."

"All right, all right. I'm going."

Kelly stepped out the front door. Diamond and Michael watched her descend the steps and climb behind the wheel of her car.

Once Kelly had driven off, Diamond said, "She's really nice."

"Hmm." Michael's tone was sardonic.

She whipped her head around to face him. "What does that mean? You don't agree?"

"No, I'm not saying that. My sister's definitely a nice person. But she's a bit too much of a drama queen sometimes. And she constantly worries about me, thinking I can't take care of myself."

"Uh-oh. I'm sensing a negative tone. Was she right when she said she thought you were mad at her?"

Michael hedged. "Mad is too strong a word. A bit annoyed, yes."

"She loves you. You can't blame her for that."

"No . . . but you've only just met her. She may be sweet, but she knows how to get her way. She's good at being able to manipulate a situation to get what she wants. Especially from me."

"She's your baby sister. They're supposed to know how to do that. Not that I could ever do that with my older sister, but maybe it's the whole male-female dynamic."

"Could be," Michael acknowledged.

"Besides, she's the only immediate family you have left. Regardless of her *alleged* shortcomings, you need to cherish her."

"I get the point." Michael slipped his arms around Diamond's waist and pulled her close. "And what do you mean, *alleged*?"

"I spent the whole afternoon gabbing with her. She seems pretty reasonable to me."

"You women—you'll always defend each other."

"Only when we know we're right."

"I didn't think women were ever wrong."

Diamond smiled. "Smart man."

"Whatever." Michael chuckled, then nuzzled his nose against her neck. "Maybe we can talk about something else."

"Hmm . . . like my car?" Diamond joked. She knew good and well her car was the last thing on Michael's mind.

He met her eyes. "Are you sorry it won't be ready until tomorrow?"

Diamond trailed a finger down the length of Michael's spine. "Very. That means I have to stay here at least another night. Goodness, what will I do with all the time?"

Michael slowly lowered his face toward hers. "I can think of something."

"Can you now?"

His lips were now a fraction from hers. She could feel his warm breath on her face.

"Unless you had another suggestion . . ."

Diamond's entire body tingled. She was enjoying this verbal foreplay very much. But she couldn't help wondering what tomorrow would bring. "Michael, what's happening between us?"

He inhaled deeply, his expression growing serious. "Something that seems to be out of our control." He pulled his head back a little, allowing them to look at each other without going cross-eyed. "And I'll be honest. I'm a little afraid. As much as possible, I'd like to take things slowly. Move one day at a time and see where things lead."

"Michael." Diamond framed one side of his face. "What is it?" she asked gently. "What's holding you back?"

Closing his eyes, Michael turned his face into her palm. She was warm and soft, and he couldn't get enough of something about her. He almost wanted to tell her. Almost wanted to let all the pent-up anguish go. Which was a profound yet shocking thought.

Last week, he never would have imagined feeling this way. No one had even begun to crack the barrier around his heart. So what was different about Diamond? The fact that she counseled people every day? The fact that her being here made him wish for the dreams he'd once had? Or was it simply time for him to finally open up about what he was feeling, as Kelly always urged him to do?

He hated that he couldn't figure out what was going on in his own mind, his own heart. The only thing he knew for sure was that ever since Diamond had come into his life, he was starting to see a light at the end of the very dark tunnel he had been in for the past year.

Still, if he took the first step and began to open up, what if he completely fell apart? That was what he feared the most, because falling apart was something he didn't want to do.

"Maybe soon, Diamond," Michael said. "But not yet."

She didn't argue with him, which he appreciated.
She said, "Whenever you're ready."

"What if I'm ready for something else right
now?"

"Oh?" Diamond's pulse accelerated. "Like
what?"

"Like . . . a walk on the beach. A *walk* this time.
We can catch the sunset, which I have to say is
really incredible."

A soft smile touched Diamond's lips. Though
they had met each other under bizarre circumstances, Michael seemed to be doing his best to
woo her. She didn't for a minute believe that his
attraction to her was purely sexual, but it was nice
to know that he was trying to make that clear.

"A walk on the beach sounds great. Let me go
get ready."

Diamond started off, but Michael took hold of
her arm, stopping her.

"Not so fast," he said. Then gave her a kiss that
held the promise of what would come later tonight.

A short while later, Michael and Diamond walked
hand in hand on the beach. Instead of carrying
their shoes, they opted to leave them in the car,
which was only a short walk from the sand.

There was a slight hint of a breeze, making their
late evening stroll quite comfortable. They were
the only two people on this stretch of the beach,
though in the distance other people walked
around. Some brave souls—no doubt tourists—
were in the water.

The sun, a brilliant orange, dipped along the
edge of the horizon over the water. It was simply
magnificent. Stopping, Diamond said, "This is so

beautiful, Michael. I never get to see the sun set over the water in Miami. Of course, Miami has great sunrises over the Atlantic." *I could get used to this place,* she added silently.

Behind her, Michael cuddled his body against hers. Her eyes fluttered shut as she savored the feeling of being close to him.

"So, you like?" he asked.

Your touch, or the view? Diamond wanted to ask. Instead, she turned to face him and said, "It's like heaven on earth. Makes me want to stay here forever."

"I've only been here a couple of times before."

"Only a couple?"

"I know. Not enough. But I'm sure this won't be the last time." Michael was slowly becoming interested in doing little things again, and he knew it was because of Diamond.

He looked deep into her eyes, and could see her longing. It matched his own. "I want to kiss you," he said.

In response, Diamond tipped on her toes, reaching for him.

Michael wanted to devour her, but mostly he wanted to relish every bit of her. So he brushed his mouth across hers ever so softly. When she sighed her enjoyment, he gently nipped her bottom lip. He moved his mouth from her lips to her cheek, from her cheek to her forehead, from her forehead to her other cheek, then finally to her nose. Diamond pressed her body against his, clearly wanting more, but Michael did everything but fully kiss her on those velvety soft lips of hers.

"Michael!" she protested. "You're making me crazy."

"Let's walk."

Once again Michael took her hand, chuckling as she groaned in frustration. He wanted her weak with need for him.

Michael led Diamond on a slow walk. He wasn't sure how far they walked, but when they stopped, the sun had completely disappeared. The beach was now dark, except for the moonlight that danced across the water.

Michael stopped walking and ran his hands down Diamond's arms. "You're cold," he said, feeling her goose bumps.

"A little bit."

He rubbed her arms vigorously to warm her. "I guess making love out here is out of the question?"

"Oh."

"If I was thinking ahead, I would have brought a blanket. I'm not too sure how fun it will be rolling around in the sand."

Diamond threw her head back and laughed. "I never thought of that, but it could get . . . challenging."

Michael placed an arm across Diamond's shoulder and turned her around. "There's nothing like a warm bed."

"Mmm. You can say that again."

"Ready to leave?"

"I've been ready for a long time."

The moment Michael and Diamond stepped into the foyer of his house, Michael swept Diamond into his arms. He kissed her hard, his tongue delving into her mouth. His hot hands were all over her, as if he couldn't get enough of her.

Urgently, he slipped the straps of her top off her shoulders, dragging the flimsy material down to above her breasts. Lowering his head, he kissed her shoulder, then gently bit her flesh.

Diamond moaned softly. She took Michael's hand and placed it on her breast. But it wasn't enough. Pulling away from him, she pulled the top over her head and dropped it to the floor.

"Oh, baby."

Michael's reaction to her filled her with a sense of power. Instead of going back into his arms, she bit down on her bottom lip, then headed into the living room.

He followed her quickly, taking her arm and whirling her around to face him. "God, you're so soft," Michael said in a raspy voice. He cupped one of her breasts. "Why can't I get enough of you?"

Diamond tore at his shirt, breaking off a few buttons in order to get the restrictive material out of the way. Her tongue nearly burned on his searing flesh as her hands struggled to undo the button on his jeans. She finally got the button open and yanked down the zipper. Lowering herself onto the sofa behind her, she pulled the jeans down over his magnificent thighs. He kicked them off.

"I love your belly button," she told him, fingering it. She leaned forward and dipped her tongue into it.

A sexual growl escaped Michael's lips.

"I could do this for hours," Diamond said, then lapped at his navel again.

"I wouldn't be able to stand it." Michael lowered himself before her. He took one of her legs into his hands, and Diamond went still, wondering what he was going to do. Dropping his mouth to her knee, he began to run circles along her leg with his tongue.

Diamond extended her other leg onto Michael's chest, her toes exploring the exposed flesh and nest of curls beneath his shirt. There weren't a lot of curls, just enough for her toes to play with. She ran her foot across his chest seductively, hoping to tease him the way he was teasing her.

Goodness, she had never known that her legs were such an erogenous zone! She wanted his tongue and hands all over her. Sighing with pleasure, she arched her back.

Accepting her unspoken invitation, Michael brought his lips to her stomach, where he dipped his tongue into the hollow of her belly button as she had done to him. He ran his fingers across her torso, molding, sculpting, causing the fire deep within Diamond's belly to burn out of control. He found her nipples and tweaked and pulled them until they were hardened peaks.

Diamond could hear the soft groans coming from Michael's lips as he kneaded her breasts with his hands. How she wanted him, to have his tongue tantalize her . . .

And then his wet tongue flicked out and laved her thick, taut nipple, sending a flood of sensations right down to her throbbing center. Relentlessly he teased her, tantalized her with his tongue, nearly bringing Diamond over the edge.

"Oh, Michael! I need you inside me." Her hands gripped his back, her nails pierced his skin, and still Michael was merciless. He was driving her utterly crazy with desire.

"Michael, please . . ."

"Here or the bedroom?"

"The bedroom's too far."

Michael scooped her off the sofa and lowered her to the thick area rug. He ran his fingers down her torso, past her belly button, to the rim of her skirt. Bunching the stretchy skirt in his hands, he pulled both the skirt and her lacy underwear off her body in one swift motion.

He took a minute to take off his briefs and retrieve a condom from his jeans. Then he was on top of Diamond, entering her. She cried out as he filled her. Diamond arched her hips to move rhythmically with him. Each thrust made her cry out in sweet ecstasy.

Their lovemaking wasn't as frenzied this time, but slow and intense, each of them savoring every moment. Michael loved her for what seemed an eternity, until finally Diamond's body contracted and she held on to him as her body spasmed from the sweetest of orgasms. One more deep thrust, and Michael came moments later.

I love you, Diamond thought, her arms still wrapped tightly around him. It didn't seem possible, but she knew it was true.

On the carpet, they lay in each other's arms until they faded into a satisfied sleep.

CHAPTER SEVENTEEN

The next morning, Michael awoke early and slipped out of bed. Diamond didn't move. She was deep in what seemed to be a comfortable slumber.

The sun had barely started to rise, but Michael got dressed, grabbed his car keys, and left the house. He had called Jacob a few times and gotten no answer. Jacob could easily be ignoring his phone as Michael often did, but for some reason, Michael had awakened with a terrible feeling about his friend in the middle of the night.

The roads were pretty clear, and Michael got to Jacob's place in just over ten minutes.

Other than the whispering of the oak trees in the soft wind as Michael stepped out of the car, the house was quiet and still.

Too quiet. Too still.

Standing in the driveway, Michael looked up at the old house. Something about it made him tremble. As if it were void of its very heart.

Michael frowned, wondering why that thought had come into his mind. But he knew. He was worried about his friend. It was nothing he could pinpoint, but deep in his soul he felt unease.

Jacob's car wasn't in the driveway, so either he had already headed to work or the old Buick was in the garage. Walking toward the porch, Michael listened for sound.

And heard none.

Suddenly, inexplicably, he felt a chill kiss his nape. The same chill he felt when his cop instincts told him something was wrong.

He quickened his pace, charging up the steps two at a time. Forgetting the doorbell, he banged on the aluminum door instead.

No shuffling feet inside, which he should have heard if Jacob was getting ready for work.

No voice calling out to him.

No sound at all, except that of two crows conversing with each other.

He pounded again, but still there was no answer.

Lord, maybe he was overreacting. Jacob had seemed tired and thin when Michael had last seen him, but that was no reason for him to think the worst now. Maybe his friend had met a woman and had spent the night there.

He hoped that was the case.

But to not answer his phone for days?

Michael turned and headed down the steps. He looked over his shoulder at the front door for a final time.

Still no Jacob.

Much later, Michael and Diamond were back at his place after having gone out for breakfast and then stopping at Roy's Repairs to pick up her car. Diamond was on edge, having learned that a strange man had gone into the shop asking about her and where she was staying in Naples. To ensure that they weren't followed, Michael let Diamond take the lead on the way back to his house so he could watch the cars behind them. From what he could tell, Clay was not in any of those cars. Michael doubted he had been around the auto shop when he and Diamond had left.

Michael and Diamond stepped into the foyer. Diamond kicked off her sandals, then placed one hand on her forehead and one hand on her hip.

"Diamond, I know you hate guns, but I think it's time I taught you how to use mine. If Clay's still around here, asking questions—"

"I don't know, Michael."

"You need to be prepared. I'm not saying he'll ever find you here, but just in case he does and I'm not here, you don't want to be helpless. I don't want you to be helpless."

Michael heard Diamond breathe in and out audibly. "All right," she said after a long moment. "Teach me."

Several minutes later, they were both outside in his backyard. Michael led her through the trees to a clear spot. "See that stump? That's what I normally use for target practice. That's why I brought these old soda bottles." He walked toward the stump and placed one of the plastic bottles on it. "I put a bottle here; then I shoot it."

"Why did you fill them partly with water?"

"Good question. I fill them with water for better balance, so that when I shoot them, they don't go flying all over the place."

Diamond nodded. "What should I do with this one?" she asked of the bottle she had carried.

"Put it in the grass for now." She did. "All right.

Come closer. I promise you, Diamond. You're not going to get hurt."

"I trust you."

"Before we get started, put these ear plugs in your ears." He dug into his pocket and withdrew two small packages that held the ear plugs. "Now." Michael pulled the gun's clip from his waistband. "Right now, the gun doesn't have its clip in. It needs to be in, in order to fire." He popped the clip into the gun. "This is a nine millimeter, by the way."

"I've never been this close to a gun before."

"You don't need to be afraid of it. Just remember, keep your arms steady, look at your target, and fire. I'll demonstrate."

Michael looked at the soda bottle and fired. Diamond jumped from shock.

"My goodness," she said. "That was so loud." Water gushed out of the bottle.

"All right. Let me show you how to do it. Come stand in front of me." Diamond did. "Take the gun. Okay, stand with your legs slightly apart and hold the gun up toward your target. See those two small black edges at the back of the gun?"

"Yeah."

"If you look through those, you'll be able to line up your target."

Diamond maneuvered the gun until she could see the bottle the way Michael had instructed. "Oh, I get it. Okay."

"Now take your other hand and hold it under your wrist. That'll give you more support as you fire the gun."

"I can't believe I'm doing this."

"Are you ready?"

"I think so."

"Okay." Michael kept his arms on her waist for added support. "Go ahead."

Diamond slowly pressed the trigger. As the gun fired, her arm pulled back. The bullet flew through the trees, completely missing the target.

"Great. That sucked."

"It was your first try. Do it again. Concentrate on your target and on keeping your arms steady."

Diamond once again fired the gun. This time, she hit the top right corner of the bottle.

"I did it!" she exclaimed in amazement. "I actually did it!"

Michael kissed her lightly on the cheek. "Good work. And not as scary as you thought, right?"

She shrugged. "No. Not really."

"Back to work, Rambo."

"Yes, sir."

The next morning, Michael was dismayed after calling Jacob three times and getting no answer. Where was his friend?

Michael spoke into the phone. "Jacob, it's Michael calling again. Give me a call as soon as possible. Okay?"

Michael replaced the receiver on the living room phone. He stood for a long moment, gnawing on his bottom lip. He was so consumed with his thoughts that when he felt the arms snake around his waist, he jumped.

Diamond giggled as he spun around in her arms. "You're up early. Sneaking out of bed to call your girlfriend?"

Michael managed only a halfhearted grin.

"It's pretty early," Diamond said. "You left me all alone . . ."

"I needed to call a friend."

Looking at him with concern, Diamond asked, "Everything okay?"

"I hope so."

Michael didn't volunteer any more information, so Diamond didn't bother to ask. "What do you want to do today?"

"I ..." He shrugged. "I hadn't thought about it. I kind of figured, now that you have your car back ..." His voice trailed off.

Diamond's eyes narrowed. "Now that I have my car back what?"

Michael slipped out of her embrace and walked farther into the living room. Frowning, Diamond followed him.

"You mean, am I leaving?" she asked.

"The thought crossed my mind."

Something was different about Michael today. Last night, they had spent another incredible night making love. But now it seemed he was pulling away again. "Well, I ... I hadn't really thought about leaving. I figured I'd give it another day to contact the police about the drug issue, see if they still want me to stick around." She paused. "You ... you want me to leave?"

"I'm sure you're ready to head back home."

Disappointment washed over her. That was a totally noncommittal answer if she'd ever heard one. She didn't expect Michael to express his undying love for her, but *some* sort of interest in whether she stayed or left would be nice.

"Sounds like you want to get rid of me."

"I know you have a life to get back to."

Stunned, Diamond gaped at Michael. "And what about what's happened between us? Am I supposed to just leave and forget about you?"

"I told you I wanted to take things slowly."

"Slowly I understand. But if I leave, are we even going to stay in touch? Or have I just made another huge mistake?"

Michael paced to the window. "I still need time."

"Time for what?"

"To figure things out. Look, I told you . . ." But he didn't finish his statement.

"Exactly. You haven't told me anything. I don't know what you're going through. You constantly shut me out."

Maybe she wasn't being unreasonable, but all Michael could hear now was the way Debra had nagged him during their last days. "It's like there's a wall between us now," Debra had said. "I don't know if you even love me anymore."

"What are you talking about?" Michael had asked. He regularly told her he loved her; he spent as much time with her and Ashley as he could.

He'd put his arm around Debra but she shrugged it off.

"Your job is more important than me. Than us."

"That's not true. Why are you saying this? Yeah, I've done a few extra duties, but we need the money because you're not working anymore. I want to give you and Ashley the best. You both mean the world to me."

"I need to get out of here."

Michael had looked at his wife in shock. "Where are you going?"

"Out," she had responded. She had grabbed her purse and not even looked back as she charged out of their apartment.

It was one of the times when Debra had started an argument with him, then left to "clear her head'' that she had come back in the middle of the night to find Ashley had died.

All of Debra's concerns about his so-called lack of affection had been lies. Michael had learned that later, when Debra had quickly moved in with a man whom he had considered his friend. Just like that, the Debra who'd supposedly cared about him opening up with his feelings was gone. She had left him for her lover, left him to deal with the death of their daughter on his own.

When he and Debra had argued, bad things happened—the worst thing being the death of their daughter. He didn't want to argue with Diamond now.

"I don't want to argue, Diamond."

"Who says we're arguing?"

"This is hardly a positive discussion."

"It could be if you'd just tell me the truth."

Michael turned from the window and hurried past Diamond. "I've got something to do."

"Oh, so you're going to walk away from me again?"

"I'll be back."

"Should I be here when you return?"

Michael paused at the opening to the living room. The sad note in Diamond's voice felt like a stab in his heart. She wasn't Debra. She hadn't betrayed him, then abandoned him.

Yet he said, "Do what you want."

Then he grabbed his keys off the hallway table and walked out of the house.

Damn the man!

He was frustrating her to the nth degree. How could he share his body with her in such a passionate, loving way, yet keep everything he was feeling locked deep in his heart?

She couldn't stand it anymore.

Hearing Michael's car drive away, Diamond stormed to the back of the house. She should get her stuff together and take off. Chalk Michael up as another mistake and move on.

Which was exactly what she planned to do—until her gaze wandered to the bedroom door that Michael had told her was off-limits.

She had respected him and his wishes all this time, but didn't she deserve a little respect? Sleeping with him had changed things, whether he liked it or not. At the very least, she needed to know what he was thinking. She needed to know what she was dealing with, because he sure as hell didn't want to tell her.

Maybe something in that room would give her some answers.

Instead of heading into Michael's bedroom to gather her belongings, Diamond went to the other room a couple of doors over. She reached for the knob, then paused. But seconds later, she made up her mind. She opened the door and walked into the room.

Her eyes scanning the room, she came to an immediate stop. Two metal shelving units on the right wall were full of bottles of alcohol. Hard liquor. Not wine or beer, but vodka, scotch, and whiskey.

But Michael had told her that he didn't drink anymore. So why did he have so much booze in here?

Diamond walked farther into the room. There was a desk by the back window and two tall bookcases on both walls opposite the desk. The room appeared to be some kind of study.

Over her shoulder, Diamond noticed a huge framed photo on the wall where the door was. She turned around to get a better view of it. It was a photo of an adorable baby girl, probably days after her birth. She was in a man's arms, but the man's face wasn't visible.

Something about the photo made emotion clog in her throat. It was absolutely stunning.

Rotating on her heel, Diamond walked to the desk. The back of a small framed photo faced her, and she lifted it. Again, it was a picture of a baby girl. In this picture, the baby was four or five months old. And while Diamond couldn't be one hundred percent sure, she would bet money this was the same baby featured in the huge wall portrait.

Michael's baby?

Could it be? Did Michael have a child?

If it *was* his baby . . . Diamond's brain worked a mile a minute. Maybe he was married, and he and his wife were having problems? Or was he divorced and his wife had left with their child?

Or had Michael been the stubborn one, the one who had pushed his very family away? He had worked for the Fort Lauderdale police, which meant he must have lived in the area. So the fact that he was now in Naples proved he had been the one to move.

Neither option made her feel any better. Because if Michael was married or involved with someone, then clearly he had lied to her.

Diamond walked around to the other side of the desk. No more photos. She inspected the large bookcase to her left. There were a ton of books, a combination of nonfiction and fiction titles, as well as another row of hard liquor. But there were no other pictures anywhere. If there was a woman in his life, no one could tell by looking in this room.

"What are you doing in here?"

At the sound of Michael's booming voice, Diamond whirled around. He was eyeing her with a cold, angry gaze.

"I told you this room was off-limits."

"I-I . . . just thought . . ." Diamond's tongue was suddenly as dry as sandpaper.

"This room is my private space." Michael stomped toward her.

Diamond fought the urge to back up against the wall. "You wouldn't give me any answers."

"So you decided to deliberately defy me?"

"I . . . I didn't mean any harm. I only wanted to learn more about you. You sleep with me; then you push me away—"

"You think that sleeping with me gives you the right?"

Diamond swallowed painfully. "Yes, I did." She met him with a hard gaze. "You shared something special with me, yet you're going through so much pain and you won't share that with me. I thought if I could find an answer in this room, I could help you."

Silence filled the air, but it was so tense, it was suffocating. Her heart aching, Diamond watched as Michael did a three-hundred-sixty-degree turn around the room.

"Did you touch anything?"

"No. Of course not. Well, I touched the photo on your desk." She paused. "She's a beautiful baby."

Michael turned away from her. Helpless, Diamond could only watch him. He didn't move, as if he had turned to stone.

But then he brought a hand to his face. A moment later, the wracking motions of his body made Diamond realize that he was crying.

"Michael."

He didn't respond.

She moved slowly toward him and placed a hand on his back. "Michael . . ."

"You keep pushing and pushing, but you have no clue what I'm going through."

Diamond felt overcome with emotion. "I'm sorry, Michael. I didn't want to hurt you. I wanted to help."

"How can you help? You can't bring her back."

A chill washed over Diamond. He couldn't possibly mean . . .

She said, "I don't understand."

Michael turned then. Tears were steaming down his face. "Of course you don't understand. How could you understand?"

"The baby . . . is she . . . ?"

"Ashley died a year ago. The anniversary of her death was last Friday."

"No." Diamond felt as if she had been punched in the gut. A beautiful little baby like that shouldn't die. "She was your daughter?"

"Yes."

Diamond covered her mouth as she sobbed. No wonder she had seen so much pain in Michael's eyes. Not only had he lived through the death of his infant daughter, the one-year anniversary had just passed.

"How old?" Diamond asked.

"Seven months. It was SIDS."

"Oh, God. Michael, I . . . I don't know what to say."

"No one ever does. Not the doctors. Not even my wife."

"Your wife?" So he was still married.

"She left me. Right after our daughter died."

What kind of woman walked out on her husband after the death of their child? "I'm so sorry you had to go through this alone. I can't imagine how awful it must have been for you."

Michael chuckled without mirth. "Oh, and it gets better. Which means worse, of course."

How could it be any worse than losing his family? Diamond extended her hand and gently placed it on Michael's arm. "Do you . . . do you want to tell me about it?"

"You really want to know?" Michael asked.

Diamond looked up at Michael with tear-filled eyes. "Yes."

"All right. And maybe once I tell you the story, you'll understand why we can't have a future."

CHAPTER EIGHTEEN

Six months earlier

Michael Robbins sat across from his captain, unable to believe what he was hearing. "Tell me this is a joke."

"Afraid not."

Michael had expected it, yet the reality was still a shock. "Suspended?"

"With pay," Jason Burgess added, as though that was supposed to make a difference.

"I don't care about the money. I did nothing wrong."

"Robbins," Burgess continued, addressing him by his surname, as was the common practice among police officers, "this is standard procedure. All cops under investigation of such a serious nature are suspended with pay."

"That guy reached into his jacket for something. How was I to know it wasn't a gun or a knife?"

"Hey, you don't have to convince me. I've been out there on the streets. I know what it's like."

"No, I just have to convince Internal Affairs, and they think I'm some sort of crazed cop who goes around killing innocent people."

Burgess frowned. "I wouldn't go that far."

"Really?" Michael challenged, rising from the chair opposite the captain's desk. "Then why are they suspending me? This is the first time I've fired my gun."

"I understand, Robbins, but he had a bottle of rum. Rum, for goodness' sake."

"I know," Michael said with chagrin. "Appleton Gold." It would have been almost laughable, if the pathetic truth hadn't been that he'd actually shot a man over a bottle of rum. "Look, I don't know why he reached for that while I was chasing him. Maybe he wanted to scare me, and he did, because all I saw was a flash—"

"And I'm sure IA will ultimately find you had just cause to fire your weapon."

"I've never fired my weapon before. Never. Hell, I've rarely pulled it out, yet IA can't give me the benefit of the doubt?"

"That's not how it works."

"No, when you're a cop, you're presumed guilty, then have to prove your innocence."

Captain Burgess rose to meet Michael. "Don't take it personally."

"It sure as hell seemed personal when they interrogated me for hours." Michael stepped past the captain to the small window. He peered through the blinds, but didn't see anything beyond the bleak, gray sky that promised a torrential downpour.

Bleak, just like his mood. Just like his life.

Burgess spoke to his back. "Look, even if they want to, IA can't just take your word for it. Despite how you're feeling now, you know that. They have to rule out any chance of foul play, especially when it isn't a cut-and-dried situation.''

Anger seizing him, Michael spun around. ''It is cut and dried. He reached into his jacket. I saw a flash. I didn't have time to see if he was going to shoot or stab me.'' Or fling a mickey or rum at his head. Drunks everywhere would be outraged, while the media would have a good laugh when this one went to trial: COP KILLS DRUNK OVER BOTTLE OF BOOZE.

''I believe you.''

The captain spoke calmly, which irritated Michael even more. If he'd at least act self-righteous, Michael could justify taking out his anger on him. But the truth was, Burgess really was on his side, so it made no sense hollering at him. ''Damn. I'm sorry.''

''It's okay.'' Burgess clamped a hand on Michael's shoulder. ''I know you're upset right now, but maybe some time off will do you some good. Give you some time to relax. God knows, if anyone deserves it, you do.''

Michael spun around. ''What's that supposed to mean?''

''It's no secret you've been going through a rough time. Sheesh, you lost your daughter. Your wife. And all you did was take a couple weeks off. Stress like that . . . it's got to affect a person.''

Michael narrowed his eyes as he looked at his captain. ''You think . . . you think I shot this guy because I was stressed?''

''I didn't say that.''

But the look on Burgess's face told Michael it was true. ''You didn't have to. God, I thought you knew me better than that.''

"Look, I don't want you gone any more than you want to be gone. You're one of my best officers. But the truth is, even the best of officers are only human. And only as good as their mental state," he added softly. "Robbins, take this time for you."

Michael dragged a hand over his face. This situation was getting worse by the second. "If you think I shot this guy because of my *mental state*, then what is IA going to think? Man, could this get any worse?"

What if he lost his job over this?

"Let's not jump the gun. This is only temporary, Robbins," Captain Burgess stressed. "As soon as IA clears you—and I have no doubt that they will—you'll be reinstated and back on the road." At Michael's skeptical frown, he added, "I know this job is your life. Hell, you didn't take much time off when others would have disappeared in a hole in the ground. But everyone needs a break sometime. That's all this is. A break."

"A break," Michael repeated, his voice flat.

"That's right."

Michael blew out a ragged breath. "You know what?" He withdrew his badge. "You can take this back. I quit."

"Whoa." Captain Burgess held up both hands. "Wait a second."

"What's the point? If you think I'm not in my right mind, then what is everyone else thinking? I don't want to be on this job if all anyone is gonna do is second-guess my every move. Hell, that's probably been happening already."

Lines creased the captain's forehead, and Michael knew the man was more than a little weary. "Robbins, you're overreacting."

"Oh, I am, am I?" Michael marched to the door.

"Robbins."

His hand on the doorknob, Michael turned back to the captain.

"Don't make this kind of decision on a whim."

Michael opened his mouth to respond, but he knew his captain was right. "All right."

Then, opening the door, Michael stepped out of the office.

Once Michael started talking, it seemed he couldn't stop.

"Instead of quitting, I decided on a leave of absence. Quoting stress and bereavement as my reasons, I asked for an open-ended leave until I was ready to return to the job. My captain was happy with that option, so it was a win-win situation on all sides.

"Days later, I moved to Naples. My aunt had once owned this house. It's still in the family for any of us to use. Sometimes my relatives from up north come down here and use it as a vacation spot when they want sunshine in the winter. But for the most part, it remains empty. Needing to get away, I decided to make this my permanent residence until I was ready to return to the job.

"As soon as I got here, I felt better. Solitude was what I wanted, a place to grieve in private. A place where no one knew me."

Michael finally met Diamond's gaze. Before now, he had been afraid to look at her. But as she sat beside him on the sofa, he saw no disappointment in her eyes. Only compassion.

He went on. "That first night—and this is the part I'm ashamed about—I found myself at a bar not too far from here. Some small, dark place frequented by serious drinkers. People there don't care how sloshed you get as long as you aren't driving. The waitresses don't ask questions that aren't any of their business, and that was fine with me.

"I spent days there at a small table in a back corner, with the only conversation from anyone being a question as to whether or not I'd like another drink. Even though I sat alone, I guess I was looking for some type of affinity with someone else. I never found that, and soon realized that I could just as easily drink in my own house and not have to worry about getting a cab home.

"The problem with turning to alcohol for relief is that one day you realize you're dependent on it. At first, I thought I'd get drunk for a few days, pass some time in oblivion to get the grief out of my system. It didn't work that way. Some days I said, 'Just one drink.' You know, to ease the pressure. 'Today, but not tomorrow,' I'd tell myself. But the next day came and the pain was as great as the day before, and I was pouring myself another drink.

"To make a long story short, it took me a good couple months to realize I needed help. I didn't want to live this way anymore. Then I met someone, a friend who had gone through heartache and had also turned to alcohol to ease the pain. He wasn't ready to change, which made it hard for me to get motivated, and I ended up drinking pretty heavily until a couple months ago."

"But if you quit—"

"I know—why do I have so much alcohol in my house?" When Diamond nodded, he continued. "It's kind of my test. A constant reminder of where I don't want to be again."

"But isn't it too tempting?"

"Not really. Maybe because I wasn't addicted to alcohol for years, I was able to stop when I was ready. I still go in that room sometimes when I'm feeling really down. And when I'm able to make it through the pain without reaching for a drink, then I know I'm continuing to make progress."

"What happened with the investigation?"

"Internal Affairs cleared me. They agreed that, given the circumstances, I couldn't have known the man wasn't pulling a weapon from his coat."

Sighing softly, Diamond stroked Michael's face. "I truly am sorry for your loss. I know it's hard for someone who hasn't been in your shoes to know exactly what to say. But I feel for you. No one should have to go through what you've suffered."

"Now do you understand why we can't have a future?"

Diamond didn't say anything. Instead, she looked away.

"I'm not saying this to hurt you. Exactly the opposite. I'll admit, being with you this week has made me start coming out of my shell—"

"See—"

"But I still have a long way to go. And I have to do that alone."

"Why?"

"It's just the way it has to be."

Diamond released Michael's hand and stood. The bad thing was, he was speaking calmly and rationally, like he knew exactly what he wanted. How could she argue with that?

"Sometimes what you think you need isn't what you really need. It's not good for you to deal with grief like this alone. Your wife may have abandoned you, but I'll be here for you, Michael."

"Your life is in Miami."

"Isn't yours? Maybe it's time you stopped running."

"I lost my daughter. I killed a man. Do you really think I can run from that?"

"I didn't mean it like that. I was trying to say that maybe if you get back into a regular routine—"

"Please," Michael said, cutting her off. "Don't tell me what I need. This has been hard enough."

Frustrated, Diamond only stared at Michael. Once again, she had come up against a brick wall. She wanted to be there for him, but she couldn't force herself on him.

She tried once more to get through to him. "When I was in high school, I met someone. Despite being very popular, he was also an introvert. The two of us connected, fell in love. We understood each other in a way that no one else did. I was so incredibly happy and thought I always would be. Then he was killed in a car accident.

"I was devastated. Depressed for months. It was like there was a dark cloud following me everywhere I went. I honestly thought I'd never be happy again, much less love again. But it does get better. It does get easier."

Michael merely nodded.

"All right." Diamond couldn't hide her exasperation. Clearly, Michael needed space. She could talk to him until she turned orange and she wasn't going to get through to him. Besides, she had enough problems of her own. Could she handle dealing with Michael's, as well?

"I'll go call the police regarding the drugs issue," Diamond told him. "And if they don't need me to stick around . . . I'll leave."

CHAPTER NINETEEN

Once learning that the police were not going to pursue charges against her, Diamond left Michael's house. But her heart ached as she did, and she couldn't stop thinking about him during her drive back to Miami.

She felt guilty for leaving, even though he had pushed her away. Surely there was something she could do for him to help ease his pain. But what?

Were the several days she had spent with him only a dream? An isolated moment in time? Lord knew, she didn't want that to be the case. She had found something in Michael that she hadn't felt since she had fallen in love with James. She didn't want to lose that.

Somehow, she had fallen in love with him.

But if the man wasn't ready for a relationship, what was she supposed to do?

That question plagued her over the next couple days, so much so that on the third day, she woke up bright and early and got in her car. She started driving back to Naples.

* * *

When Michael's doorbell rang early that morning during breakfast, he knew.

Hadn't he known for a few days? Known in the place deep inside where people could sense these things?

Like before, he felt helpless. Helpless and disillusioned because he hadn't been able to prevent it. Another person he'd cared about was forever gone.

He knew in his soul that Jacob was dead.

The doorbell rang again, and he gripped the edges of the wooden chair in the kitchen so hard that his hands actually ached.

But not even the pain in his hands would assuage the anguish in his heart.

The doorbell rang a third time, and he stood. What point was there in not answering the door, in pretending that it hadn't happened?

So he started his walk down the hallway. And braced himself for what he knew he was going to hear.

Diamond couldn't explain it, nor could she shake the feeling, but the closer she got to Naples, the more convinced she was that something horrible had happened.

When she reached his small home, she saw that his car was parked in front of the house. The bumper was still dented from where she'd hit it, making her remember the incident that day—and all that had followed—but that now seemed so long ago.

She parked her car behind his, but didn't get

out right away. Suddenly, she was afraid. What if he didn't want to see her?

Closing her eyes, she counted to ten, then decided to go for it. That's why she was here, after all. She opened the door and got out, then walked determinedly to the front door. But once there, she paused, suddenly unsure of herself.

Do it. Knock on the door. If Michael wanted nothing more to do with her, if all that had happened between them was simply a dream that would never come true, then she had to know.

Her stomach knotted at the thought. God help her. Let that not be the case. Not now that she'd fallen for him.

Before she lost her courage, she raised her hand to the door and pounded on it. She waited at least a minute before knocking again.

After another minute passed, she wondered why he wasn't answering the door. Was he okay inside? She reached for the knob. It turned.

The first thing that hit her was the stench of alcohol. Vodka maybe, or scotch. She wasn't sure, but the scent hung in the air, vile and overbearing. Her heart sped up as she hurried into the house, wondering what had happened.

And then she saw him.

Out cold on the living room sofa.

Her stomach lurched.

"Oh, my God!" Diamond scrambled to Michael's side. "Michael! Michael!"

Wracked with fear, she grabbed his wrist to check for a pulse, all kinds of horrifying thoughts playing out in her mind. But Michael began to stir, letting her know he wasn't dead.

"Michael," she repeated, not as loudly this time. Michael didn't open his eyes. "He's dead . . ."

"Who's dead?"

"I knew something was wrong. I called. I went by. I called again. I never heard from him."

"Who?"

"Jacob."

"Who's Jacob?"

"The friend I told you about. The one I used to drink with. The police came by this morning. He hadn't gone to work for days. God, I should have known."

Diamond glanced around the living room. That's when she saw the broken glass on the floor beneath the window. "Michael, have you been drinking?"

Diamond groaned when he didn't respond. She stood and marched to the kitchen where she filled a glass with tap water. She returned to him moments later.

"Michael," she said sternly. "Drink this."

He sat up, took the glass, and placed it on the coffee table. "You think water is going to solve my problems?"

Diamond ran a hand over his head. He flinched, and she recoiled as though she'd been stung. Why wouldn't he accept her comfort?

"If you've been drinking, you need to hydrate yourself."

"I haven't been drinking."

"I can smell the alcohol."

"Maybe in the room, but not in my mouth." He opened wide for her to sniff. She did, not detecting any scent of liquor.

"Feel better?"

"There's no need for your snide tone. What was I to think? I walk in here and smell alcohol. You told me you had abused liquor . . ."

"Not anymore."

"You threw a bottle against the wall?"

"What are you gonna do—arrest me?"

This conversation was getting her nowhere, so Diamond decided to change the subject. "When was the last time you ate?"

"Who cares?"

His answer alarmed her. Concerned, she looked into his eyes. What she saw caused a chill to sweep over her. They were void of any emotion.

He truly didn't care.

"Your friend wouldn't want this," she said, hoping to get through to him. "He'd want you to take care of yourself."

"How would you know?"

"Because no one would want this for you."

Michael huffed. "I forgot. You're a quack psychologist."

Diamond winced at his comment, but somehow she managed to bite her tongue. He had just lost his friend and was lashing out at her because she was a convenient outlet for his pain.

"Don't shut me out, Michael," she said to his back, because he was now standing by the window. "I know it hurts, but—"

Turning, he faced her, a cloud of anguish marring his beautiful features. "I want to be alone."

"I'm not leaving you."

"You may as well do it now. Sooner or later, you all leave."

Was that what he thought? That she would leave him? Didn't he realize how much she cared for him?

"I'm here because—"

"Go." He didn't shout the word, but the intensity with which he said it made her jump.

"I love you, Michael."

"Don't waste your time."

This was not the reaction she'd expected when she first told him that she loved him. Her heart felt as if it were going to split in two. She stepped toward him, reached out to touch his arm. He stepped away from her.

"I'm no good for you. I'm no good for anyone. Not now. Maybe not ever."

How could she get through his wall of pain? Her arms ached to hold him, comfort him, make all his pain disappear. But every time she took a step toward him, he moved away. "I don't believe that."

"Please just go."

A tear rolled down her face. "All right," she said softly. "I'll go."

"Good."

Drawing in a deep breath, she brushed away the tear. "I'll call you later."

"Don't."

His jaw had hardened once again, and the look in his eyes was deadly serious.

Unable to stomach the look, Diamond turned and headed for the door. Somehow she made it to her car without breaking down.

And somehow she made it home, though she cried her eyes out all the way there.

Michael felt like crap when Diamond left and he still felt like crap hours later.

He hadn't wanted to be so cruel, but he'd had to do what was necessary to make her leave.

I love you.

He winced. Her unexpected proclamation of love had shocked him, and he hadn't known how to deal with it.

Part of him had wanted to reach out to her, but the other part, the part immersed in grief, had held him back. Pushing Diamond away was the best gift he could give her. Nothing in his life lasted for long. He'd lost Keith in Desert Storm. Both his parents had died at once. Then his sweet baby girl had been taken from him. He could deal with Debra's leaving, as long as he still had Ashley in his life.

He didn't want to despair, but how could he deny the reality that long-term happiness had always eluded him?

It could be different with Diamond.

With her around, he had started to hope. Something inside him still wanted to believe that there was good in the world, that he could be happy with that one special person.

But Jacob's suicide had shattered all those hopes.

The police had come by because there had been a note for him in Jacob's place. Jacob had simply written, "I miss Merline terribly. She was the love of my life and I want to be with her again. I'm sorry, Mike."

"I'm sorry, Diamond," Michael said softly. "I wish things could be different."

Clay couldn't do this anymore.

He had been back and forth between Miami and Naples a few times now, hoping to find Diamond at the radio station or luck out and see her driving on the road. So far, he hadn't had any luck.

He needed to do something else. Something that was going to get him the results he wanted.

Clay glanced at his watch. It was a quarter to five. He knew the radio station's receptionist would be heading out of the office within twenty minutes. He also knew which car in the lot was hers. He had watched her get in it more than once.

The Sunbird was probably ten years old. It would be a piece of cake to break into.

Clay pulled his ball cap down over his face and got out of the car. He dropped his cigarette butt onto the asphalt and ground it out with his sneaker. Then he quickly glanced around before jogging across the street to the parking lot.

Minutes later, he was in the car. Waiting for the receptionist.

"Don't say a word."

The receptionist screamed as she realized Clay was in the backseat of her car. He almost laughed— her reaction was priceless.

"You're gonna drive till I tell you to stop."

"Oh, God. Please don't hurt me!"

"If you listen to what I have to say, you'll be just fine. But if you don't, I have a gun, and believe me, I'll use it if you force me to."

"Oh . . ." the woman moaned.

Her hands shook as she drove, but she managed to get them far enough south and west that they reached an undeveloped area of Dade County.

"Pull into this parking lot." It belonged to an out-of-service gas station.

She did as told, though she now started sobbing.

"Kill the engine and pass me the keys."

"Wh-what are you gonna do to me?"

"That depends on what you tell me." Clay ran a hand along the woman's neck.

"What do you w-want to know?"

"How can I find Lady D?"

"Lady D?"

"Yeah," Clay snapped. Anger started to fill his veins. "Don't act like you don't know who she is!"

"N-no. Of course. Yes, I know who she is."

"Well, I want to know how to find her. She hasn't been at work."

"I don't know where she is."

Clay's hand tightened around the woman's throat. "Wrong answer! That is not what I want to hear."

The woman gasped, saying, "All right. Please . . ."

Clay loosened his grip. "You have one more chance, before I crush your throat."

"She lives in Coral Gables."

"Where?"

"What are you gonna do to her?"

"You're making me angry."

"She's my friend. . . . I don't want you to hurt her."

Clay squeezed the woman's throat until she choked and wheezed. He wanted to kill her, but he needed her alive.

He slowly released his hold on her. In a hoarse voice she said, "Okay. Okay."

"What's the address?"

The woman started to cry. "I don't remember the exact address."

"But can you tell me how to get there?"

She whimpered. "Yes. She lives in an apartment complex called Still Waters."

When the receptionist finished giving Clay the information he wanted, he patted her on the head. "Very good." He looked around and saw no one in the immediate area. "Now get out."

"Out?"

"Yeah, I'm letting you go."

While she got out the front, Clay got out from the back. Within seconds, he was behind the wheel and starting the car.

The woman hugged her torso, crying. He knew she'd go to the cops. She could promise him she wouldn't, but that would be a lie.

So as he reversed the car, he sped up, ramming into her. He smiled with satisfaction when he saw her body go flying, then land in a limp heap on the ground.

CHAPTER TWENTY

The rain fell in a steady rhythm, much like Diamond's tears.

"I'm sorry," Tara said. "I know I sound like a broken record, but I don't know what else to say."

Diamond and Tara sat on Tara's bed. Darren was in the living room, giving them both some privacy.

Hunched forward, her face buried in her hands, Diamond moaned. She didn't remove her hands completely, but made an opening for her mouth so she could speak. "Tara, I feel like a fool. I hadn't even talked to him, just got in my car and drove for two hours until I reached his place. Only for him to tell me to leave."

"From what you say, he's in a lot of pain."

"He knew what he was doing when he pushed me away. I told him I loved him and he said something like 'Don't waste your time.' What am I to make of that?"

"You said you both truly connected. Maybe he just needs some time."

A half moan, half sob escaped Diamond, and she threw her head backward, closed her eyes. "It wouldn't have been so bad if he didn't give me that . . . that look. Like he had no feelings whatsoever for me. I practically begged him not to shut me out. But he basically told me we didn't have a chance at a future."

"That's why you have no choice but to give him the space he needs. Let him call you when he's ready."

"And if he doesn't?"

Silence filled the room. The soft pitter-patter of the rain against the window seemed like miniature exclamation points emphasizing the hopelessness of the situation.

Tara edged across the bed and wrapped Diamond in a hug. "If he doesn't, then I'll be here for you. You're strong, Diamond. A survivor. You'll get through this."

Sniffling, Diamond brushed away her tears.

"You know you're staying here tonight," Tara said. "Given the state you're in, and with Clay still on the loose, there's no way I'm letting you out of my sight."

Diamond knew there was no point in arguing. Besides, she didn't want to. There was nowhere else she would rather be right now.

The night's sleep had worked magic for Diamond. This morning, she felt much better, even optimistic. And she didn't look as wretched as she had yesterday. The brightness for which she'd earned her name had returned to her eyes.

Her appetite had also returned, which was definitely a good thing. Now, as Diamond and Tara sat at the patio table in the backyard, Diamond took the remains of her third fried dumpling and ran it along the surface of the plate, soaking up the juices of the ackee and salt fish. Darren had prepared the Jamaican breakfast, and Diamond was very impressed.

"No wonder you married Darren. A man who can cook like this. Mmm."

"Girl, I know that impresses you simply because you can't cook."

"I can cook."

"But only you can eat it." Tara smiled sweetly at her.

Diamond sighed. "Michael can cook, too."

"Don't think about him. Remember, today is going to be a happy day."

Diamond nodded. "You're right. And please forgive me for yesterday. I wasn't myself."

"There's nothing to forgive."

Diamond sipped her coffee, then met Tara's eyes. "I was such a mess."

"And I was a mess when Harris dumped me. You were there for me then. That's what family does. We're there for each other."

The rain had continued well into the night, leaving the earth with a fresh, damp smell. It was a smell that made Diamond think of new beginnings. Fresh starts. Especially beneath the warm sun that now kissed the earth.

Tara was right. If Michael didn't love her, then she would get through this. She would move on. Diamond would tell her callers the same thing.

"I'm thinking about going back to work," Diamond announced. "Maybe tomorrow."

Tara looked at her with alarm. "What?"

"It's what I do, Tara. I miss it."

"Sure you miss it. But don't you think that's a hasty decision? I thought you wanted to keep a low profile until Clay was caught. I mean, if you were still at Michael's place, would you be heading back to work?"

"No," Diamond admitted, her heart aching at the memory of the mostly wonderful days she had spent with Michael. "But I'm not at his place. And come tomorrow, when you and the rest of the world heads back to work after the weekend, I don't want to be sitting at home alone, moping."

"I understand that. But don't make this decision for the wrong reasons. I think it's too soon."

Diamond finished off her coffee. "I haven't made up my mind. I was also considering staying away another week, and if nothing happens, then heading back."

Tara nodded her understanding. "Let's hope Clay gets caught in the meantime."

"He's a smart guy, but maybe he'll make a mistake. Get caught speeding or something."

"You can stay here for the week if you want," Tara offered.

Diamond shook her head. "You've got a husband you need to spend time with. You don't need me here as a third wheel."

"Darren won't mind."

"Thanks, but no, thanks. Clay doesn't know where I live."

"So you want to be a willing target?"

"No, but . . ." Diamond blew out a weary breath. "I can't put my life on hold forever, either."

"Diamond." Tara reached across the table and squeezed her hand. "Just be careful."

"I will."

* * *

"You dolt. I can't believe you let her walk away!"

Michael rolled his eyes, thankful his sister couldn't see through the phone line. "I didn't call you for a lecture."

"Well, someone's got to talk some sense into you. Diamond is the best thing to happen to you in a long time, and you pushed her away."

"It wasn't going to work."

"Why? Because you're so hell-bent on living in your self-imposed hell? For goodness' sake, if you're going to be a martyr, at least let it be for a good cause."

It was two days after Diamond had left, and Michael had only called his sister because she'd left numerous messages for him. It seemed that despite what she said about leaving him alone, she couldn't keep her word. "I'm not ready for another relationship. At least not now."

Kelly groaned long and loud. "It's a good thing you're my brother, or honestly, I'd be tempted to strangle you."

"Kelly, I want you to listen, and listen good. I'm not sure I'm ever moving back to South Florida. I like it where I am, and I think I'll be here for a long time."

"You're joking, right?"

"I'm dead serious."

"What about your job?"

"I can find something else to do."

"So you want to push everyone away, is that it?"

"I didn't say that."

"No, but you're isolating yourself. Day by day, you keep slipping away. And I'm not sure there's anything I can do to help you anymore. Michael, that breaks my heart."

Kelly's voice broke, and Michael felt his insides twist into a painful knot. "Kelly—"

"No. You don't need anyone, remember? I'll keep that in mind the next time I get the foolish notion to call you and see if you're okay."

Then Kelly hung up.

Michael held the receiver to his ear for a long time before finally replacing it on its cradle.

The ringing phone woke Diamond up early Monday morning. She had left Tara's place last night close to midnight, and by the time she had gone through all her mail and Internet e-mail, it was minutes after two in the morning.

Diamond lifted her head to look at the bedside clock. Twelve minutes after nine. She dragged a pillow over her head, ignoring the phone.

The ringing stopped, but less than a minute later, it started again. This time, Diamond sat up and reached for the phone. Maybe it was Michael.

"Hello?"

"Diamond, thank God. It's Ken."

Ken, her station manager. His tone made her stomach sink. "What is it? What's happened?"

"It's Marnie."

Marnie was the radio station's receptionist and a friend. "What about Marnie?"

Ken released a sad sigh. "She's in a coma."

"No," Diamond said, horrified.

"She was found on the west side of Kendall Friday night, in a pretty remote area. But her car was parked in front of the station, which means someone moved it, because she always parks in the lot."

Ken paused. "She'd been run down. Left for dead."

Please, God. Let this be a nightmare. "Who did this?"

"We don't know."

Suddenly, Diamond felt nauseated. "But you think it was Clay."

"Yeah, that would be my guess. Of course, it could be anyone."

"It was Clay," Diamond said, certain of that fact. "He wanted to get to me. God, I'm so sorry. If I'd been around, this wouldn't have happened."

"You don't know that."

"The guy's a nut. He was frustrated because he couldn't get to me. So he went after a substitute. Marnie must have been the first one to get in his path." Diamond moaned. "How bad is she?"

"Her husband says she's in pretty bad shape, but the doctors are hopeful."

"I'll have to give Eric a call."

"He's at the hospital."

"Jackson Memorial?"

"Uh-huh."

"I have to go visit her."

"I'm not sure she can have visitors yet."

"Maybe not. But I have to do something."

"Right now, all anyone can do is pray."

CHAPTER TWENTY-ONE

Diamond wanted to call Michael and tell him what was going on, but she didn't. He was going through his own issues and didn't need her to worry about in the process.

If he would worry.

Instead, Diamond called Tara and her parents, told them what was going on, then tried to allay their concerns. "Come stay with us until this madman is caught," her mother had said.

"I can't do that," Diamond had replied. "He's already hurt someone I care about. I don't want to put anyone else in danger."

"Baby, we are so worried about you."

"I know. But I'm going to be okay."

Diamond had tried to sound confident for her family, but she wasn't so sure. Clay was completely unpredictable, and probably even angrier than the first time he had attacked her.

After calling her family, she spent a couple of hours at the hospital with Eric. She hadn't been able to see Marnie, but she at least felt good being able to offer Eric comfort. And while Diamond blamed herself, he didn't blame her. At the end of the visit, they had prayed for Marnie's healthy recovery.

Now, Diamond was heading back to her place. She was stuck in traffic along the Palmetto Expressway, something that normally irritated her, but today she didn't mind at all. She wasn't even sure she wanted to head home. Where would she be safe? Eric had told her that the police had no clues as to who had hurt Marnie. The doctors had ruled out sexual assault, which only made Diamond even more convinced that Clay had been responsible for the attack.

Close to an hour later, Diamond was off the highway and nearing her apartment complex when she saw her gas gauge. It was almost on empty. She pulled her car into a Mobil gas station. She kept her Mobil Speedpass in the glove compartment, so she opened it to retrieve it.

Then gasped in horror.

Diamond stared, disbelieving. There was a gun. On top of the gun was a piece of paper. Pulling out the paper, she saw that it was a note.

The note read:

Diamond, I knew you wouldn't take this gun if I offered it to you, so I decided to put it in your car. I want you to have it, just in case. Don't be afraid to use it if you have to.

Michael

Diamond's breath came in ragged spurts. When had Michael put the gun in her car?

She couldn't help it—she felt touched. Even

though he had pushed her away, he had still been thinking of her. Still been thinking of her safety.

Maybe she should give him a call.

She didn't like the idea of the gun being in her car, but she was actually thankful for it. Given what had happened to Marnie, she might very well need it.

Diamond retrieved her Speedpass, got out of the car, and filled her tank. All the while, her body was tingling from a mixture of anxiety and excitement.

As nervous as she was, she would give Michael a call. Just as soon as she got home.

Just a little while longer.

By now, Clay was used to waiting. But at least now, he could see a light at the end of the tunnel.

Thanks to that wuss from the radio station, he now knew where Diamond lived. His persistence had paid off. He had consistently checked the apartment complex parking lot until he found her car. She must have come home sometime during the night because her car was in the lot this morning.

Once he had spotted the car, Clay was no longer tired. He had become wide awake with anticipation, excited over what was to come next.

Then, when he had seen her, he had hardly been able to control himself. He had wanted to run from the car and grab her right there. But other people had been around, and the last time he had tried to grab her with people around, he had failed.

As he watched her drive off, another idea had come to him. One that was simply brilliant. He had seen which apartment she had come from. All he'd had to do was head inside.

It hadn't taken him long. And he knew it was meant to be, because Diamond hadn't activated her alarm. So stupid.

It was payback time.

Finally.

Diamond opened her door and stepped into her apartment. She kicked off her shoes, then wriggled her toes. Turning, she activated her alarm in the stay-at-home mode. If anyone tried to get in, the alarm would sound.

She sighed sadly. When had it come to this? The better question was, when would it be over?

The answering machine on the nearby counter was blinking, indicating that Diamond had at least one message. She walked the short distance to the machine and hit the play button.

"Diamond, hi. It's Kelly, Michael's sister. I talked to Michael, and he told me what happened, and I just want to say—don't give up on him. He's going through a really hard time, and I can't even get through to him. Believe me, he's not normally so dense. I know he cares about you." She paused. "Anyway, that's all for now. You have my number. Call me when you get a chance. Oh, and I hope that freak is caught soon. I'm keeping you in my prayers."

The machine beeped, indicating there were no more messages.

Well, how nice of Kelly to call. But the message made her reconsider her decision to phone Michael. Not that she didn't want to, but it would probably be a good idea if she spoke with Kelly first.

Which she would do, right after she took a shower.

Diamond turned.

Instantly, her body froze.

Clay was standing outside the door to her bedroom!

"Diamond." A slow smile spread on his face. "You've finally come back to me."

Diamond's heart spasmed in her chest. She was steps away from the apartment door, and if she was smart, she would turn and flee. But Clay would chase her, and she might not be fast enough.

Why, oh, why hadn't she taken the gun from the glove compartment? Michael's words about having a gun for protection hit home. He was right. Oh, Lord, he was right.

"You've been very bad, Diamond." Clay sauntered toward her. The look on his face was entirely too smug, as if he knew he had her right where he wanted her.

"H-how did you g-get—"

"You can't run from me. When are you going to learn that?"

"I-I . . ." Diamond couldn't get any other words past her lips.

Clay now stood directly in front of her. He reached for her and trailed a finger down the base of her neck to right above her cleavage. Diamond shivered in disgust.

"God, Diamond. I've missed you so much." He ogled her chest. Then his eyes flew to hers and hate filled them. "I wanted things to work out. But you've betrayed me."

"No," Diamond quickly said. This man was more

deranged than she had ever thought. What kind of fantasy world was he living in if he thought they had a chance of a relationship?

"I saw you." Clay spoke through clenched teeth. "I saw you all over that guy!"

Diamond took a step backward. "You mean in Naples?"

"You know exactly what I mean."

Clay wouldn't get out of her space, and Diamond backed up until she was pressed against the door. *God, help me,* she said silently. *I need to get out of this situation.*

Suddenly she was saying, "The guy you saw . . . he's a cousin. I-I went to Naples to . . . to visit him. He . . . he's been sick."

"He didn't look sick."

"Depressed. His baby died," Diamond continued, weaving truth into her story. "I went out there to make sure he's okay."

Clay's eyes flitted around. Diamond could tell he was thinking, trying to determine if she was telling him the truth.

"You know I would never run from you."

"I don't know if I should believe you."

As much as it killed her to do so, Diamond placed a palm on Clay's cheek. "Believe me, Clay. I . . . I care about you."

His eyes took on a glazed look. "You do?"

"Of course." She swallowed. "But sometimes . . . sometimes you scare me. You can get so upset."

"That's because . . . I thought you betrayed me with that guy."

Diamond nervously glanced around. What could she grab?

Nothing.

She couldn't stay trapped in this apartment with

Clay. She had to get out. Getting out of here was her only chance.

"Are you nervous, Diamond?"

She thought about lying. In the end, she said, "Yes, I'm nervous. It's been so long."

"Are you happy to see me?"

"Of course I am."

"Then prove it. Make love to me."

Diamond did everything in her power to keep from physically shaking. God help her, she didn't want to have sex with Clay. Not even to save her life.

She would much rather take her chances running out of the apartment. Bruises and scrapes would be better than having to deal with Clay in any intimate way.

"What's the matter, Diamond?"

"Um . . . I . . . I *want* to. But I don't have any protection. And we're just getting back together. You don't want to risk pregnancy, do you? Maybe one day, but not yet."

Clay's eyes narrowed on her.

The gun was in her car. If she could get to it . . .

"Let's go to the drugstore and get some condoms."

"You want to leave?"

"Both of us. Together." Thank God she had activated her alarm. She had a special distress code that she could input which would deactivate the alarm, but allow the police to know that she was in trouble and needed help.

Diamond forced a smile, then leaned forward and kissed Clay on the cheek. "Don't you want to make love to me without any worries? Let's get a twelve-pack, because I want to make love to you until the early hours of the morning.''

As Clay mulled her suggestion over, Diamond held her breath. Then he said, ''All right.''

Relief flooded her.

Diamond grabbed her purse, then turned to the door. She pressed in her distress code. Maybe outside she could stall Clay until the police came.

''Open the door, Diamond,'' Clay told her.

Diamond opened the door and cautiously stepped outside. She looked around but didn't see anyone. She had always loved this place because it was a quiet apartment, but now she wished she lived somewhere busier, like Miami Beach.

She killed as much time as possible digging into her purse for her keys and locking the door.

''Let's go.''

Diamond managed a jerky nod. Clay placed his hand on the small of her back and together they descended the stairs. ''How far is the drugstore?'' he asked.

''It'll be a short drive in my car. Um, do you want to drive?'' If she could get into the passenger seat, she could grab the gun.

''No. You drive. I don't want you jumping out of the car.''

Diamond chuckled nervously. ''Why would I do that?''

''I just want to be sure.''

As they walked to her nearby car, Diamond bit down hard on her cheek. *What now?* If she got into the car, could she try and get the gun? With her in the driver's seat, Clay would certainly have a better chance of getting it than she would.

Don't get in the car. The voice was so clear, it was as if someone had spoken to her.

"Um, let me open your door for you." Diamond went to the passenger side, unlocked, then opened the door. The glove compartment was right there. She had to take a chance.

Her hands trembling, she reached for the glove compartment.

"What are you doing?" Clay demanded.

Open, open. C'mon, open!

The glove compartment popped open.

That's when she felt the blow to her head.

CHAPTER TWENTY-TWO

Wincing from pain, Diamond fell forward but quickly tried to turn herself onto her back. If she could get onto her back, she could kick. If she could get onto her back, she could grab the gun and be in a position to fire it.

But Clay grabbed hold of her feet and started to drag her from the car.

Screaming, Diamond reached into the glove compartment on her way out. Her fingers closed around the gun.

But as her chin and head hit the car's frame as she was pulled violently from the car, she lost hold of the gun and it toppled to the asphalt.

With all her strength, she struggled to get her feet free of him. She got one leg free and wriggled onto her side. Clay dragged her, her head scraping across the hot asphalt. Diamond continued to kick, and somehow she got free.

As fast as she could, she scrambled to her feet. She turned, saw the gun, and ran for it. But Clay caught up with her before she reached it, snaring her around the waist. He whirled her around, banging her back against the car with lethal force.

Diamond cried out in pain. But she didn't let the pain hold her back. She reached for Clay's face, scratching it. One of her nails hit his eye, and she dug into it.

Clay cried out as he punched her in the face. The punch nearly knocked her head off, but Diamond quickly rebounded, working a leg up to knee him in the groin.

At last he released her. Diamond dove for the gun.

Her fingers closed around the handle . . .

Clay kicked it from her and ran for it.

And in that moment, her entire life passed before her eyes.

She had failed. She was going to die.

"Freeze!"

In disbelief, Diamond angled her head over her shoulder. Relief washed over her in waves when she saw several Miami-Dade police officers standing with their guns drawn.

"Drop the weapon!" one of them yelled.

Diamond's eyes flew to Clay. He stood with the nine millimeter in his hands.

"Drop it!"

Instead of dropping it, Clay slowly raised it. Slowly aimed it in her direction.

When Diamond heard the explosion, she thought for sure she was dead. But when she realized that she was screaming uncontrollably, she knew she was still alive.

She lifted her head and once again looked in Clay's direction. He was sprawled on the ground.

Arms lifted her from the asphalt. It seemed as if a million questions at once were fired at her, but she couldn't decipher one of them. Her eyes were fixated on Clay. Blood oozed from his chest.

"Ma'am, are you all right?"

Diamond turned to face the officer who was speaking to her. Then she collapsed in his arms.

Except for some scrapes and bruises and aches and pains, Diamond was okay. The paramedics had checked her out at the scene and pronounced her healthy.

But the very best part was that Clay was dead.

Diamond didn't wish death on anyone, but Clay was a dangerous psychopath. He'd nearly killed Marnie, he had tried to kill her, and if he ever got out of a mental facility again, he would surely hurt someone else.

Now she was at her parents' place, surrounded by her mother and father, Tara and Darren. Her mother insisted that she lie on the sofa covered in a warm duvet. They wouldn't stop fussing over her.

"Here's some chicken soup," Tara said.

"I don't have a cold."

"You're welcome."

Diamond sat up. "The point is, I'm fine." Her eyes misted as she remembered the day's scary events. "At least I will be now."

"It's a horrible thing to say," Tara said. "But I'm glad he's dead. He can never hurt you or anyone else again."

"I know."

Sitting on the sofa's armrest, Diamond's father stroked her head. "I'm glad someone killed him. Or I would have had to take care of that myself."

"Me and your father," her mother chimed from the nearby kitchen. "No one could hurt you like

that and get away with it. Not while your mama
still has breath.''

"It all ended the way it was supposed to end,''
Darren piped in. "That's what's important. Having
to go through another trial . . .''

"Ain't that the truth.'' Diamond blew out a ragged breath.

Her father stood. "Let me get you a pillow.''

"Dad . . .'' But he was off.

Tara was sitting on a chair in front of the sofa.
She reached for and squeezed Diamond's hand.
Quietly she said, "Do you want me to call Michael?''

Diamond shook her head.

"Don't you think he should—''

"No. I don't need anyone's pity. Least of all his.''

"I think he'd want to know.''

"If he calls me, I'll tell him. But for right now,
all I need is what I have right here. My family.
People who I know care about me.''

Two days later, when Diamond returned home,
she heard Michael's message on her answering
machine.

"Diamond, I heard what happened. Thank God
you're okay. I'm sure you're taking it easy, but
when you're up to it, please call me. We should
talk.''

Diamond's stomach tingled with nerves. Kelly
must have seen the story of her attack on the news
and called her brother.

Which was why he'd called her. She held no
illusions that he had called her because he was
ready to accept the love she wanted to give him.

But, against her better judgment, she returned

his call. She was disappointed to get his voice mail. Regardless, she left him a message.

"Michael, I got your message. Thanks for calling. I don't want you to worry. I'm doing perfectly fine. I have my family; thank God for that." She paused, deciding what to say next. "I would love nothing better than to talk to you. However, I don't want to talk to you because you feel pity for me over what happened. I want to talk to you when you've made your decision, when you know in your heart that you're ready for a relationship with me. Or that you're not. But I don't want to talk to you while you're still confused. While you're still running from your grief. I mean it, Michael. Don't call me unless you know what you want. Please, take care of yourself. And I hope to hear from you soon."

Michael didn't return her call.

CHAPTER TWENTY-THREE

"This is Lady D, your host of *The Love Chronicles* on Talk 93, South Florida's hottest talk radio station."

Diamond paused briefly. "I thought long and hard about what the topic for tonight would be, and I've decided I'll keep it open. Call me and talk to me about whatever you want. Any aspect of your relationships. But first—I know you have some questions for me, so I want to share my own story.

"As most of you know, I've been away for a while. If you saw the recent story on the news, then you know what I've been going through. Of course, not all of you will have seen it, so I'm going to share the story with you.

"Over two years ago, a man named Clay Horton became obsessed with me. He was straight-up crazy, and after trying to abduct me, he was locked up in an institution for the criminally insane. However, a month ago, he escaped, and I wasn't about to sit around and wait for him to come find me. I took off. Unfortunately, I learned that while you can run, you can't hide.

"This man might have been crazy, but he was cunning and smart, and made my life a living hell until two weeks ago. He attacked me again, and this time . . . this time, I wasn't sure if I was going to make it."

Diamond blew out a long breath. "I called on God, and no doubt, He heard my prayer. I escaped with only some bruises. Emotionally, I needed to lie low for a while, but now I'm ready to get back to work. Because if there's one thing I learned, it's that you can't let the bad things that happen in life hold you back."

Diamond thought of Michael. Her throat clogged with emotion. When she hadn't heard from him, part of her had wanted to stay in bed forever and sleep away the pain of having given her heart to yet another wrong man. But another part of her had wanted to put the whole ordeal behind her and move on.

That hadn't been easy, but she knew that being back at work was a step in the right direction.

"Live each day with purpose and drive," Diamond continued. "Live it like it's your last. Perhaps that's why, during a time when I least expected it, I fell in love.

"Yes, love. Here I was, running from a crazy man, and I fell in love. But this is my whole point about not letting the bad things that happen in life hold us back. The man I fell in love with has lived through some very trying times, and while I know that in his heart he has a lot of love to give, he wasn't ready. Now, I understand where he was coming from, so I don't hold that against him. Not too long ago, I was also afraid to give my heart because of pain from the past. But in a strange way, meeting this man helped me let go of all that. Maybe that's why I was supposed to meet him. Maybe that's why I was supposed to fall in love with him, even if it wasn't meant to last.

"So, what do I do now? I go on, continue to work, and continue to have faith that for the most part, we're all good people. I'm living for today. Yesterday is over, and tomorrow may never be mine. But I have today."

Diamond smiled sadly. "All right, I've rambled enough. I'm going to open the phone lines now. Call me and speak to me about whatever's on your mind." She rattled off the numbers for Broward, Dade, and Palm Beach Counties.

It was going to be a long night, but she was glad to be back here. Glad to be starting her routine again.

Michael listened to the tape his sister had sent him with a mix of fear, sadness, and excitement. He could be angry with Kelly for once again interfering in his life, but he wasn't. How could he be angry with her when he knew that she was simply looking out for him because she wanted him to be happy?

And hearing Diamond's voice again . . . it was like going home.

Her voice was one thing, but her words were another. There was no denying that she was talking about him. Talking about how she had fallen in love with him.

In love . . .

Michael dropped his head back on the pillow and groaned loudly. His brain could deny it all day, but his heart knew the truth—he had fallen in love with her, too. Since the time she had left, he had been more miserable than he had been in a long time, mostly because he had wanted to reach out to her but felt crippled. He wanted to love again, but he was so afraid to do so.

But Diamond's words about life—how there were no guarantees, how one shouldn't let bad things hold one back—struck a chord with him. She was right. And deep inside him, there was a small spark of hope that wanted to burn brighter. Indeed, it had burned brighter—until Jacob's death had put him on a downward spiral.

The only thing Michael knew for sure was that he didn't want to spend the rest of his days living this way, with a cloud of darkness hanging over him forever. He wanted sunshine.

He wanted Diamond.

But he remembered her words on his answering service. She'd told him not to call her until he was ready, until he knew without a doubt what he wanted.

He knew what he wanted, but there was still some letting go he had to do. Other loose ends to tie up before he made that call. Things to arrange—like going back to work.

She had been gone for three weeks. It might take him another three weeks, but he was determined to be the man Diamond needed him to be the day he called her to tell her what was in his heart.

One month later

"This is Lady D, your host of *The Love Chronicles* on Talk 93, South Florida's hottest talk radio. Tonight, we're discussing limits. What will you put up with from your mate? What won't you put up with? Call me and share your opinions." She paused, looking at the display to see who would be her next caller. "I've got Michael from Miami on the line. How you doing tonight, Michael?"

There was a moment of dead air, and Diamond was ready to hit the dump button when she heard, "Hi."

That voice. A tingling sensation spread all through her body. Could it be?

She went on as she normally would. "Hey, Michael. What are your limits? Anything you've put up with that you wish you hadn't?"

"It is so good to hear your voice again."

Dear God, it *was* him. Calling her during her live show! Diamond was suddenly so flustered, she almost couldn't speak.

She wanted to continue her job as host, treating Michael like a typical caller. But as her heart filled with joy, it took control, making her say, "It's good to hear your voice, too."

"I missed you."

"Michael." Her eyes fluttered shut. "Why are you calling me here?"

"I wanted to surprise you with all of South Florida as my audience, so you'll forever have my words to you on tape. And I also wanted to talk about limits."

"Okay."

"I realize I've been limiting myself. Limiting my potential for happiness. I heard one of your broadcasts from some time ago, where you talked about not letting bad things from your past hold you back. And it got me to thinking.

"That's exactly what I was doing. I don't know

. . . maybe I needed all this time to heal. But I'm finally ready to go on. I don't want to limit my happiness anymore. And that's why I wanted to talk to you.''

Diamond's heart was beating so loudly, she was sure her audience could hear it. ''Michael, you'd better spell out what you're trying to say. I don't want to jump to any conclusions.''

''All right. I'm in love with you, Di—Lady D. And I hope I haven't done my best to push you away.''

''Well, you *did* do your best,'' Diamond told him. A smile had crept onto her face and tears filled her eyes. ''But you didn't do a good enough job. Because I left my heart in Naples when I left you.''

The phone lines were flashing out of control, and in the opposite room, Rick, her producer, was grinning at her widely, holding two thumbs up.

''Thank God. I promise, I am going to take good care of it. I want to see you as soon as possible. Tonight, even.''

Diamond didn't want to wait another moment to see him. So much time had already been lost. ''Michael, will you hold the line? We have to take a commercial break.''

''I'll do anything for you.''

The moment the commercial began, Diamond tore off her headpiece and covered her face in both hands. Had this really just happened? She felt giddy and nervous, as if she were dreaming.

''That was great!'' Rick exclaimed, running into the room. ''Our listeners are going to eat this up.''

Diamond couldn't care less about the ratings, though she was pleased this drama made for good radio. She cared about seeing Michael, about throwing herself into his arms and kissing him until she was breathless.

She put her headpiece on again and answered Michael's call on a private line. "You still there?"

"Of course."

"Where are you?"

"About ten minutes away."

Her heart slammed against her chest. "You're coming to see me?"

"That's the plan. Unless you don't want me to."

Diamond glanced at the clock. She had another twenty minutes to go before her shift ended. "Wait for me in front of the station."

"Will do."

"I can't wait to see you, Michael."

"I can't wait either, baby."

He was standing outside his vehicle, which was parked only yards from the front door of the radio station. Seeing him in the flesh, knowing he was really there, made Diamond's body grow warm all over.

She couldn't help herself. She ran toward Michael and jumped into his arms.

He caught her and whirled her around and around while she screamed in delight. Slowing down, he released her, letting her body slide down his.

She looked up at him, and he brought his lips down on hers. He kissed her like he couldn't get enough of her. He held her like he wanted to meld their bodies together.

Finally, Diamond broke away. "What are you doing here?"

"I meant what I said on the radio. I thought

about my life, my limits, how I've hampered my own happiness. I'm ready to put all the pain behind me. I want to concentrate on the future."

Smiling, Diamond gently stroked his face.

"I've moved back," Michael continued. "I'll be working on the force again."

"Oh, Michael. I'm so happy for you."

"It feels good to be back here." He stroked her chin. "It feels like I've come home."

"You have."

"I have now. Now that I've found you."

"Oh." Diamond's eyes misted. She hadn't known she was such a romantic.

"I've wasted a lot of time, but I don't want to waste another second. Will you marry me?"

"Marry . . . ?"

"Yeah. No one has ever made me feel the way you do, Diamond. Your love . . . it liberated me. I know now that what I had with Debra wasn't real, so I can put that behind me." He blew out a sharp breath. "As for Ashley . . . I'll never forget her. She'll always be in my heart. But I know she wouldn't want me to spend the rest of my days being sad over what happened. She'd want me to honor her by continuing to live." He paused. "And by giving her some sisters and brothers."

Diamond brought a hand to her chest. "Oh, my. Sisters and brothers?"

"Yeah. I was thinking ten."

"Ten!" Diamond exclaimed.

"What—you want more?"

She threw her head back and laughed at that. Then, she stretched up on her toes and planted a soft kiss on Michael's lips. "How about we start with one and go from there?"

"Sounds like a plan."

"Then kiss me. Make it official."

Michael did just that, and Diamond knew that what he'd said was true for her, as well.

In Michael's arms, she had finally come home.

Dear Readers,

After making you wait for the conclusion to Diamond Montgomery's story, I hope you truly enjoyed it! She went through some trials and tribulations to get the man she loved—and to escape danger—so I'm sure you'll agree her happy ending was well deserved.

My next BET story will feature someone you met in *In A Heartbeat:* Kelly Robbins, Michael's sister. In her story, *Fool For Love,* she is reunited with the one man who broke her heart back in high school—Ashton Hunter. Will they be able to find lasting love this time around?

I love to hear from you, so keep your letters coming. You can reach me by snail mail or e-mail.

E-mail me at: kayla@kaylaperrin.com

Or send regular mail to:
Kayla Perrin
1405 Upper Ottawa Street
#10-121
Hamilton, ON Canada
L8W 3Y4

Until next time, happy reading!

Kayla

FOOL FOR LOVE

PROLOGUE

Ten years earlier

Hotter than sin. Bracing her hands on the edge of the pedestal sink, Kelly Robbins giggled as she stared at her reflection in the bathroom mirror. *Sinfully hot. Hot, hot, hot.* She giggled again. Though relatively inexperienced in the love department, she knew that something as explosive and pleasurable as what she had enjoyed last night could only be described with those words. Last night's event was, quite simply, the best experience of her life. Now she truly knew the meaning of "out of this world."

Closing her eyes, she licked her bottom lip, remembering—experiencing again the delightful sensations as last night played in her mind. She hadn't known what to expect, whether reality would live up to fantasy. For months, she had dreamed about it, and last night her dreams came true. Finally, she had made love with Ashton

Hunter, and it had been wilder than any of her most secret fantasies.

She opened her eyes, let her gaze roam over her forehead, down the length of her face to her chin, down to the base of her neck, finally resting on the fullness of her breasts. No doubt about it, she was a different person now than twenty-four hours ago. Even her reflection was different. Her lips were fuller, sexier. Her eyes were brighter, her face more mature. She was vibrant. Her reflection said she was no longer a child. Now, she was a woman.

Ashton's woman.

Her breasts tingled at the thought, remembering the way Ashton's hands and mouth had caressed every inch of her body, bringing her to a height of ecstasy she had never dreamed possible.

With a fingertip, Kelly traced the outline of her lips, lips that were still swollen from Ashton's kisses. Her eyes grew serious. Yes, last night had been incredible, but there was so much more to what she and Ashton had shared than the physical enjoyment. Last night, through the ultimate physical intimacy, their emotional connection deepened. With each drugging kiss, with each heated caress, Ashton had shown her the depth of his love in a way he had never been able to verbally express.

And Kelly was lost. Head over heels in love.

The shrill ring of the telephone interrupted her thoughts. Excitement washing over, she darted from the bathroom into her bedroom. Ashton said he would call today, but she hadn't expected him to call before noon. Not after getting to bed so late last night.

But maybe, like her, he had found it hard to concentrate on sleep.

Though her heart danced with anticipation, she

let the phone ring three times, not wanting to appear too anxious. She lifted the receiver just before the machine picked up, and in her sexiest voice said, "Hello."

"Don't tell me you were still sleeping? Whoa, that must have been *some* night."

Her excitement faded at the sound of her best friend's voice, not Ashton's. "Karen, hi." She sat on the bed. "What's up?"

"You're asking *me* what's up? Come on, Kelly. Don't keep me in suspense. The last I saw of you at the grad party, you were sneaking out with Mr. Drop-Dead Gorgeous himself. Inquiring minds want to know."

"Hmmm . . . you mean Ashton?" Kelly asked shyly, knowing exactly whom her friend meant.

"Of course I mean Ashton! Ashton Hunter— the most wanted guy in the senior class. The one *you* left with. And let me tell you, almost every other girl at the party was green with envy! Especially Taleesha Harper. I promise not to hate you as long as you tell me every last detail. So come on. Tell me what happened!"

Smiling, Kelly lay back onto the pillows. Ashton was hers, and everybody knew it. She pinched herself to make sure she wasn't dreaming. "What can I say, Karen?" She paused for effect. "Last night was . . . the best damn night of my life!"

Karen's high-pitched squeal nearly deafened Kelly. "I knew it! Girl, I'm *so* happy for you!"

"I still can't believe it. I mean, I knew our relationship was getting more serious, but when Ashton asked me to leave with him last night . . ." Kelly sighed, contented. "Karen, he loves me. He really does."

"I am *so* jealous."

"What about you? How did your night go?"

"Malcolm got drunk and forgot I existed. But that's okay. I still had a great time."

"There'll be other men in college," Kelly assured her. "Tons of gorgeous men who will be lining up to go out with you."

Karen chuckled. "I certainly hope so, 'cause I am through worrying about Malcolm." She paused. "But what happens now? With you and Ashton, I mean. You're moving any day."

Kelly frowned, then rolled over onto her stomach. She didn't want to think about her pending move. Last month, her father had surprised her with the news that his job required he move to Fort Lauderdale, Florida—half a world away. It would have been hard enough leaving Karen, but after what she had shared with Ashton, she knew she couldn't leave. Not now, when she was happier than she'd ever been.

"I don't think my father will mind if I stay here for college," Kelly finally said, hoping she was right. "At the very least, I have the rest of the summer with Ashton. And if necessary, we can always visit each other."

"I guess you're right," Karen said.

Kelly glanced at the digital clock radio, noting that she had been on the phone with Karen for over five minutes. "Karen, let me call you later. I'm expecting Ashton's call."

Four hours later, Kelly was still waiting for that call. Her stomach was a ball of knots as she sat cross-legged on her bed, chewing on a fingernail. With each minute that passed, she grew more uneasy. Why wasn't the phone ringing? Had Ashton forgotten his promise to her? How could he, after what they shared? No, he must be sleeping, exhausted from their night together. Either that or extremely busy.

An hour and a half later, Kelly could wait no longer and decided to call Ashton. Maybe they could get together tonight, experience once again what they had last night.

"Hello, Mr. Hunter," Kelly said when Ashton's father answered the phone. "It's Kelly. Can I speak to Ashton, please?"

"Ashton . . . ?" If Kelly wasn't mistaken, he sounded puzzled. "Um, Ashton's not here, Kelly."

Something's wrong. "Do you know when he'll be home?"

Silence. Then, "Didn't Ashton tell you?"

The skin on the back of her neck prickled as a sickening feeling spread through her body. "Tell me what?"

"Ashton's gone, Kelly."

Mr. Hunter made "gone" sound final, like forever. But that couldn't be true. "Gone? I don't understand."

"Brother. I can't believe he didn't tell you, Kelly. Ashton left this morning. He got a job out west for the summer, and after that I'm not sure he's even coming back."

The room spun. Her ears rang, drowning out the sound of Mr. Hunter's voice.

Gone. For the summer. Maybe not coming back. It couldn't be true. Ashton wouldn't leave her like this, not after what they shared last night. Not without saying good-bye.

". . . tell him you called if I hear from him," Kelly heard Mr. Hunter say.

She couldn't speak. Quickly, she replaced the receiver, Mr. Hunter's words playing in her mind over and over again.

Her brain searched to make sense of the words, to explain what was clearly inexplicable. But as Kelly collapsed onto the bed, her body finally going numb, she knew that Mr. Hunter couldn't be mistaken.

Ashton had left her. Without looking back.

SIZZLING ROMANCE BY
ROCHELLE ALERS

__HIDEAWAY	1-58314-179-0	$5.99US/$7.99CAN
__PRIVATE PASSIONS	1-58314-151-0	$5.99US/$7.99CAN
__ JUST BEFORE DAWN	1-58314-103-0	$5.99US/$7.99CAN
__HARVEST MOON	1-58314-056-5	$4.99US/$6.50CAN
__SUMMER MAGIC	1-58314-012-3	$4.99US/$6.50CAN
__HAPPILY EVER AFTER	0-7860-0064-3	$4.99US/$6.50CAN
__HEAVEN SENT	0-7860-0530-0	$4.99US/$6.50CAN
__HIDDEN AGENDA	0-7860-0384-7	$4.99US/$6.50CAN
__HOME SWEET HOME	0-7860-0276-X	$4.99US/$6.50CAN
__VOWS	0-7860-0463-0	$4.99US/$6.50CAN